A WORLD
FOR
JOEY CARR

A WORLD FOR JOEY CARR

David Roth

BEAUFORT BOOKS, INC.
NEW YORK / TORONTO

No character in this book is intended to
represent any actual person; all incidents of the
story are entirely fictional in nature.

Library of Congress Cataloging in Publication Data

Roth, David.
A world for Joey Carr.

Summary: En route to his grandparents in Vermont
in search of some answers, a lonely teenage hitchhiker
meets a dying woman on her own fervent quest.
[1. Friendship—Fiction] I. Title.
PZ7.R7275Wo [Fic]   81-3879
ISBN O-8253-0058-4   AACR2

Published in the United States by Beaufort Books, Inc.,
New York. Published simultaneously in Canada by
Nelson, Foster and Scott Ltd.

Design by Ellen LoGiudice
Printed in the U.S.A.   First Edition
10 9 8 7 6 5 4 3 2 1

*For my daughters Katherine
and Sheila—traveling into
their own worlds of magic*

Author's Note

I have taken certain liberties with the
New England countryside described in
this book. Some of the towns mentioned
do not exist under the names that are used
here. Some of the roads, lakes and mountains have also been tampered with.
Abaddon Woods exists, but I'm not saying
exactly where; and whether or not Hannah Adams's friends are real or imaginary
is for the reader to decide. In every way,
though, I have remained true to the spirit
of the region I know well and call home.

Part One
THE CITY

1

Joey Carr left the park Friday at four o'clock after running three miles on the gray cinder path that wound by the broken cement benches, under the ancient trees. The sun blazed through a thick haze above the park that summer afternoon. The shadows under the trees wavered in the heat.

In his solitary run Joey had passed hundreds of people but noticed none of them. He was a thin, blond boy of fourteen, and he ran his miles with his pale-blue eyes looking steadily ahead at the path in front of him, his mind drawn inward, as in meditation.

"Thanks," he told the street vendor who had watched his shirt while he ran. He put the shirt on, but did not button it.

The vendor, an old man with only two fingers on his left hand, sold pretzels every day on the streets at the edge of the park. He mopped his face now with a dirty red handkerchief.

"Maybe someday you'll return the favor and take some pretzels home to your family," the vendor said. "After all, if I go out of business, you'll have to trust your shirt to the riffraff."

Joey grinned and dug into the pocket of his cutoffs. "I only have forty cents."

"For you there's a special today, two for the price of one."

Joey handed him the coins, and the vendor tapped his forehead in a vague salute. "Thank you, young man. Your generosity has saved me from financial ruin." He wrapped two of the hot pretzels in paper. Joey squeezed them into his shirt pocket.

"I have to go."

The vendor waved the hand with two fingers. "I'm crushed. Perhaps I'll see you tomorrow?"

Joey laughed and ran across the street. As he buttoned his shirt, the pretzels burned sticky and hot against his chest.

The streets of Cambridge were filling with people going home from work. Joey darted nimbly around them on his way back to his building. His hair, which was long and scraggly at the best of times, hung heavy and damp on the back of his neck. He wanted to take a shower before his father or Betty got home.

He let himself into the foyer and rode up in the elevator. Their apartment was near the top of the building, on the tenth floor. Betty was already there when he arrived.

Since the bedroom door was open, he tapped on it and leaned in to say hello. He stopped short when he saw that she was packing.

"Hello, Joey," she said. "Been running?"

He nodded. Her eyes were red and puffy. "What's wrong?"

She shook her head. She had long, mouse-brown hair, a

small, oval face and over-large eyes that seemed capable of reading all your secret thoughts, until you realized that without her glasses, she was nearly blind. Joey liked her the best of his father's friends, better than any of the others since his mother had died two years ago.

"What's wrong?" he repeated.

"Well, as you can see, I'm packing." She seemed about to say something else, then changed her mind and shook her head again. "Do you see my glasses anywhere around here?"

Joey found them on the bureau and handed them to her. She put them on, then closed the suitcase and put it with two others on the floor.

"Stop staring at me, Joey," she said.

All the good feeling from his run had left him now, and Joey felt as if he were shrinking inside a room suddenly grown too large for him. He didn't want Betty to leave. She had brought laughter into the apartment, a gaiety he and his father hadn't shared since his mother's death. For two years Joey and his father had lived like strangers in the same apartment, each mourning alone. Betty had brought a new relationship to them, a kind of bridge. She was someone they both liked. . . .

"Don't go," Joey said.

She looked around the room as if to see if she had forgotten anything. She avoided his eyes. Out in the living room, she searched the bookshelves. The drapes were open; light glared in from the balcony. But the room was cold, the air conditioner on full.

"I have to leave," Betty said at last.

"Why?"

"It's none . . ." Betty started to say. "No, it does concern you. I came into your life, not just your father's." She walked

13

over to him and ran one hand through his hair. "God, you're wet. Why don't you take a shower before you catch cold in here?"

He shook his head. "Why are you leaving? Did I do something?"

She made a sound that might have been a laugh. "No, Joey. It's between your father and me."

"What is?"

She looked startled by the tone of his question. "Don't be angry with him, Joey."

"What did he do?"

"It's more what he hasn't . . ." She shrugged her thin shoulders. "Sometimes people like me ask for more from a relationship than is there. Your father gives what he can. If that's not enough for me, maybe that's my problem."

"I'll talk to him. I'll . . ."

Betty laughed and hugged him. "You're sweet, Joey. Do me a favor?"

"What?"

"Don't grow up to be like your father. Stay open and warm the way you are now. Don't close down, don't play it safe." She pulled back and held his shoulders as she looked at him. "Promise me, Joey?"

He nodded.

"Call me a cab?"

He went to the telephone and made the call. Betty walked to the balcony doors and looked out at the city. Beyond her, Joey could see the traffic crawling bumper-to-bumper beside the river.

"It's funny," she said when he had completed the call. "When I first saw this apartment of yours, I thought it was a palace. A luxury high-rise with a view of the river and all of

14

Boston's lights at night. Who could ask for anything more?" She turned from the balcony. "Just me, I guess." She laughed. "Never satisfied."

He stood there.

"Come on, Joey. Give me a kiss. I'll wait for the cab downstairs."

"I'll go down with you."

"No way, Joey. No way."

When she was gone, struggling through the doorway with her three suitcases, refusing his help, he stood by the balcony doors watching the traffic. His sweaty clothes grew cold and clammy. Finally he turned off the air conditioner and took his shower. He put on a clean pair of jeans and his favorite shirt. Back in the living room he opened the doors to the balcony and went out. He was still out there when his father came home from work.

"Damn it, Joey!" his father shouted. "I've told you a hundred times not to let in all that hot air. It will take all night to get this place comfortable again."

Joey heard his father switch on the air conditioner. "It's nice out here," he said.

"What?"

"It's nice out here!"

"Well, get back inside anyway. And shut those damn doors."

Joey took one last look at the streets below, softened now by the early shadows. The haze was thickening into dusk, swallowing up the sun before it could set. Across the river, some of the lights were coming on already.

"Joey!"

He stepped into the living room and closed the doors

behind him. His father was in the kitchen, taking cold chicken, salad, and beer out of the refrigerator. Joey stared at his back.

"Betty's gone."

His father said nothing. He was reaching up into the cupboards for plates.

"Dad, Betty's gone. She left with her stuff this afternoon."

"I know."

"You knew she was going and you didn't try to stop her?"

"Sure I tried to stop her."

"I bet!"

His father turned to face him. "And what's that supposed to mean?" He was blond like Joey, but everything else about him was in contrast to Joey's thin, runner's body. Short and muscular, with large, powerful hands, he was only lately getting soft around the middle, and he still projected a strong physical presence.

He was not a handsome man, in Joey's opinion. Neither of them had the good looks that everyone admired on television. But Joey had already realized that in real life people often responded immediately and positively to someone like his father, someone who could walk into a room and, just by being there, make everyone turn and look.

Joey often felt overwhelmed by his father's aura of power. He did not think that he compared well with him, although he was secretly glad that he had inherited his own looks from his mother's side of the family. Her father, Granddad Webster, was tall and thin, a distinguished-looking gentleman in the photograph on the shelf in the living room. Joey hadn't seen him since his mother's funeral, but he remembered him as soft-spoken and wise.

His father now was staring at him. "Betty wanted to leave.

I tried to talk her into staying. I'll miss her as much as you will." There was no emotion in his voice. He might have been reading aloud the program notes in a television magazine.

"Why did she go?"

"Basically, Joey, it's none of your business."

"I live here, too."

"Sure you do. But when I'm ready to ask your advice on my love affairs, I'll let you know."

All the bitterness that had been welling up inside Joey since Betty's good-bye spilled over now. "How can you call them love affairs when you don't love anyone?"

For a moment Joey thought his father was going to hit him. Instead he turned back to the preparations for supper. "Go set the table."

Joey almost wished his father *had* hit him. Anything would be better than the way his father withdrew behind that wall. Without Betty's bridge of love, they were already slipping back into the vacuum in which they had existed for the two years since his mother's death.

Joey set three places at the table in the dining nook and waited for his father to comment on it. But they ate in silence, Betty's place at the table totally ignored by his father. When Joey cleaned up after the meal, he carefully replaced her clean dishes in the cupboard and with elaborate gentleness placed her knife, fork and spoon back in the silverware drawer.

17

2

They settled down in front of the big color television in the living room to watch the Red Sox throw away another game. Beyond the balcony, lighted signs flashed in Boston across the river. By the time the game was into the fourth inning, his father had finished the six-pack of beer he had started with supper and had poured himself a whiskey over ice. It was Friday, the start of the weekend, and his father was reverting to his old rule: beer during the week, whiskey on weekends.

His father never talked about his drinking. It was something they both watched from the sidelines as it waxed and waned, but they never discussed it. Joey had inferred his father's rule by observation. But while Betty lived with them, his father had stopped drinking whiskey altogether.

"You miss her, don't you?" Joey asked. On the television screen the Yankees were clearing the bases with a double into the gap between left field and center. His father sipped his drink.

18

"Let's not talk about it, okay?"

The Red Sox were losing by ten runs by the sixth inning, and his father was on his second whiskey. The chatter of the announcers only seemed to draw the silence in the room around them more tightly.

"How was work today?" Joey asked.

"Okay."

"Will the new line of amplifiers be ready on time?" His father was plant manager for a small stereo company in Cambridge.

"How did you know about that?"

"I heard you telling Betty."

"We'll be on target with them."

Yaz struck out with two men on base. The sixth inning was over. His father got up to pour another drink.

"Why don't you just bring the bottle over to your chair?" Joey asked softly.

His father had gone to the kitchen after ice. When he came back, he stood behind Joey's chair. "I'm going to bed."

Joey didn't want to sit there alone. "Come on, Dad, the game's not over yet."

"They're down by ten runs, Joey."

"Yeah, but they can still pull it out."

"Maybe another inning," his father said as he sank down into his chair.

Joey could feel them slipping back into the old patterns, into the way they had lived before Betty. He tried to interest his father in the ball game, but the Red Sox were no help. They gave away two more runs in the seventh inning on an error and a pop fly that dropped behind second base.

"Is it because of the way Mom died, because she was killed by muggers and no one lifted a finger to help her?"

"Is what because?" his father asked sleepily.

19

"Is that why you can't get over it?"

"I'm over it."

"Sometimes I think you won't let yourself feel anything because you don't want to feel anything about her." Joey waited for his father to explode.

"Knock it off, Joey. There's no sense raking up the past."

"Don't you see what's happening?"

"No, what's happening?" His father's voice was flat, the words a little slurred.

"We sit here like zombies. It's like before. We're going back to the way it was before Betty came."

"You have a good life, kid," his father said. "Everything you want."

"Sure." The television flickered in a blur before him. The room was spinning, his heart was beating loudly. "I'm going to write Granddad and Gram Webster, see if I can visit them this summer. Maybe I'll stay there."

Joey waited, but there was no response from his father. He was asleep, snoring softly.

"Dad?"

The snoring continued.

"Dad, I hate you." Joey stood up. "Do you hear me, Dad? I love you."

Joey gently took away his glass, then covered him with an afghan from the couch. After switching off the television, Joey went to his bedroom. In the left-hand drawer of his desk, under a pile of school papers, was his stash of money. He took five dollars, then tiptoed past his father to the door. He rode down in the elevator to the streets below.

At night the streets of the city were Joey's magic roaming ground. When things were bad at home, he took to the streets and walked for hours. He headed now toward

Harvard Square and the noise and crowds he knew he would find there.

On the way he ducked into a pinball arcade and played the machines awhile, running up indifferent scores. He couldn't concentrate. His thoughts were scattered like the flashing lights of the pinball machines. He buried himself in the heart of the crowd, but he was so alone, he jumped when someone called his name.

"Hey, Joey!"

He turned and saw Coke Pennyworth, a boy he knew slightly at school. "Hey, Coke. How's it going?"

Coke shrugged. He was heavier and taller than Joey; but without the lean strength that running gave Joey, he seemed soft and half asleep. He had a can of soda in his hand.

"Want one?" he asked.

Joey shook his head. "No, thanks."

"Where's Larry?"

"Summer camp."

"Seems funny, seeing you without him."

"Why?"

"I mean, you're always together."

Joey shrugged. "Not always."

"I mean, you're real good friends." There was envy in Coke's voice. He drank from his can of soda. Around them the pinball machines winked away, a bombardment of lights and noise.

"What are you doing this summer?" Joey asked. He looked out toward the street.

"Nothing much. Hanging around. What about you?"

Joey looked at Coke's eyes. They were wet, unfocused. "I'm going up to Vermont, to visit my grandparents. Might stay there."

"Really?"

21

Joey nodded.

"In the mountains?"

"In the Northeast Kingdom. They live by a small lake in Carverville."

"Yeah?"

"A few miles from the Canadian border."

"Must be cold up there all year."

"Not really." Joey had only been there once, years ago with his mother on a visit. But he remembered fields of wild flowers, and the little lake waves rolling onto the gravel beach.

"And you're going to live there?"

"Maybe."

"With your dad?"

Joey shook his head. "I got to go." He edged toward the doorway onto the street. "See you around."

"But when are you moving?"

"In a week or two," Joey called back to him.

The night was still hot, loud with traffic and the sounds from thousands of open windows. Instead of continuing on to Harvard Square, he turned toward home.

He hadn't lied to Coke. Despite all the confusion he had felt in the arcade, he had made up his mind. He would write to his grandparents and invite himself up for a visit. He imagined they were lonely, too—his mother had been their only child. He would make himself so useful doing chores, they would be glad to ask him to stay. They would wonder how they had got along without him.

3

Dear Granddad and Gram Webster,

Hey, remember me, Joey? I'm sorry I haven't written much, but school keeps me kind of busy. But now it's vacation.

How are you both? I hope you are well. How is the lake? I think about it a lot. I only got up there to your place once with Mom and I guess I was all of seven or eight, but it made a real impression on me.

One reason I'm writing is to see if maybe I could come up for a visit this summer. Dad and me need to get away from each other for a while. I'll explain when I see you. Hope I can come.

                                        In the meantime, love,
                                                    Joey

He folded the letter carefully and addressed the envelope. Outside his bedroom, his father still slept in his chair before the dark television. It was after midnight. Joey turned out all the lights and came back to his room. He put the letter into one pocket of his jeans. He would mail it tomorrow.

As he lay half asleep in his bed, he imagined the lake beside his grandparents' house in Vermont, the deep blue-green he remembered. But thoughts of Betty intruded, and he saw again how she had looked while telling him good-bye. He turned away from the memory to escape into dreams.

When he got up late Saturday morning, he put on his running clothes. His father was at his desk beside the balcony doors.

"Want to run with me?" Joey asked.

His father shook his head. "I've got production reports to go through."

"Well, you used to run with me. That's the only reason I asked."

"Thanks. Maybe some other time."

"You have to keep at it regular, you know." Joey wanted to stop talking about it, but he couldn't. "You can't run a couple times a year and figure you're in shape."

"I know, Joey." His father slammed down one report and picked up another. "Why don't you just go run and feel virtuous for both of us?"

"I'm not . . ."

"Joey, shut up!"

Joey nodded and left the apartment, wondering why he couldn't stop until he made his father angry.

It was another hot day. He walked quickly to the park, warming up and stretching for his run on the way. The pretzel vendor was in the shade at the east side of the park this morning, and Joey hurried over to leave his shirt.

24

"Ah, Mr. Marathon is here." The old man took Joey's shirt and draped it over one wheel of his wagon. "You want to bring some hangers, I could put up a rack to hold all your clothes."

"Thanks," Joey said and jogged toward the cinder path. Thoughts of his father were turning about in his mind as he began to run his three miles; but after one circling of the park, he was into the running itself, feeling the heat as an ally, a friend, loosening his muscles and bringing a blank forgetfulness. The trees swung by overhead, casting islands of shade. People were gathered on the benches in groups of three or four, their lips moving soundlessly as he passed. The running filled him with a sense of purpose, a feeling of order in his life.

He ran more than his three miles, not wanting to stop, not wanting to reenter the world. But at last he slowed to a walk and crisscrossed the grass until he had regained his wind. Now he could hear the conversations around him; now the trees, their magic gone, looked ragged and diseased, leaves blasted by the sun, no longer providing oasis of sweet shade. Joey retrieved his shirt and walked home.

The apartment was empty. His father had gone out without leaving a note. Joey took a shower. When he pulled on his jeans, he saw the envelope addressed to his grandparents. He found a stamp in one of the drawers in his father's desk and pasted it on; but then, instead of running out to mail the letter, he replaced it in his pocket. He was reluctant to mail it, as if there were some reason to wait, to put it off, as if he were waiting for his father to notice and say, no, don't go.

He fixed himself a ham sandwich and drank a glass of milk. After lunch he wandered around the apartment waiting for his father to return to see if he could interest him in a movie. The living room was already taking on a neglected air. His father's cup sat on his desk, half full of cold coffee. Yesterday's newspaper was scattered across the couch and two chairs. The telephone was on the floor.

At two o'clock Joey gave up waiting and went out. He spent the afternoon in the air-conditioned dreamworld of the pinball arcade. If there were people there he knew, he didn't see them, so intent was he on the path of the balls, the flash of the lights.

Late in the afternoon as he was leaving, he bumped into a Gypsy girl. Her long skirt was dirty, her low-cut blouse too tight. She followed him out onto the street.

"Read your palm, boy?" she called to him. "Tell your fortune?"

He stopped and looked back at her. Taking this as a yes, she grabbed his hand. Before he could snatch it away, she was leading him into the shelter of a boarded-over storefront. People passing by looked in at them, then hurried on.

"I only have a couple quarters left," Joey told her.

"Let's see, boy."

He dug into his pocket and took out the coins. She reached for them, but he pulled them away.

"Read my palm first."

She was dark-skinned and pretty, her hair black as midnight. As she examined his hand, he stole a look into her eyes. They were dark and liquid.

She had started an ordinary description of his life line when suddenly she stopped. She closed her eyes. A shiver ran through her body. She dropped his hand as if it were on fire.

"What is it?" he asked.

She tried to dart by him, but he stopped her. "What do you see?"

She shook her head.

He pressed the two quarters into her hand. "Please tell me."

She began to recite a nonsense verse in a strange, singsong voice:

> *"Quath vardi sat*
> *la perwith bat*
> *the perry worwith*
> *pealing pith."*

She shivered again as she went on:

> *"Soon in your life*
> *with two you'll deal.*
> *One will die,*
> *the other reveal."*

"What does that mean?" he demanded.

"No!" she cried and broke away from him. He followed her onto the street, but she quickly ran through the traffic and disappeared. He recited to himself the last few lines of her verse, before he could forget them. He shook his head. They made no more sense than the gibberish that had preceded them.

He had intended to mail the letter to his grandparents, but the Gypsy girl's strange fortune had stolen his mind and the envelope was still in his back pocket when he reached the apartment.

27

His father had not come home. Joey was tempted for a moment to go downstairs to the underground garage to see if his father had taken the car, but then decided not to. Whether it was there or not, he still wouldn't know where his father had gone or when he would be back.

Instead, he heated up a frozen dinner and watched the news on television while he ate. Then he turned off the air conditioner and opened up the balcony doors.

An hour later he took more of his money from the stash in his desk and went to a movie. On the way home, he treated himself to a hamburger and an ice-cream cone. But the more things he did to please himself, the more empty he felt. He saw lights on in the apartment as he walked toward the building, but as he let himself in upstairs, he realized he had left them on himself.

"The hell with this," he said aloud. His voice startled him in the silence of the apartment. He went back down to the street and mailed the letter to his grandparents in the mailbox on the corner. Whatever he had been waiting for hadn't happened.

Upstairs again, he sat out on the balcony and watched the lights across the river flickering and flashing. It was like a giant pinball machine, so big you couldn't see who was playing.

He sat there for hours. Just before dawn, he fell into a shallow, uneasy sleep.

4

The sound of the apartment door opening awakened him. The sun was already up, a bloated orange ball slashed in half by a bank of early-morning clouds. Joey rubbed his face, looked into the living room, and watched his father tiptoe in. He had been dressed for a night on the town, but now his tie was hanging loosely around his neck and his jacket was rumpled, as if it had been walked on along the way. He didn't notice Joey on the balcony until he reached for the knob on the air conditioner.

"Oh, you're up already," he said.

"Sort of."

"Come in so I can close the doors." His father's voice was flat and tired. Joey came inside and watched him shut the balcony doors and draw the drapes. In the gray light they could barely see each other.

"Good party?" Joey asked.

"Yeah. Look, Joey, I'm going to crash for a while. Need anything?"

"No. I'm going to run."

His father was already heading for the bathroom. "When you come back, keep it quiet as you can, okay?"

"Yeah." Joey went to his room and put on his running clothes. They were still damp from yesterday's run and were beginning to smell. He put them on anyway. On the way out, he slammed the door behind him.

The streets were empty, washed by a Sunday-morning hush. Alone in the city, he felt his mood lighten. There was a magic to the streets at this time of day, and, unlike the romance of the night streets, he didn't have to share this morning magic with anyone.

He was halfway through three miles around the park when he heard a terrible yelping behind him. A small dog, hardly more than a blur of brown fur, bounced against his legs as it sped by. A split second later the lethal arrow of a Doberman followed. The smaller dog tried to take cover in a grove of trees, but the Doberman had caught him. By the time Joey raced over, the dogs were a whirl of legs and teeth.

Joey knew the Doberman would make fast work of the smaller dog, leaving him maimed or dead. City dogs gave no quarter. Joey grabbed up the short end of a broken branch and waded into the fight.

It was hard to see where one dog ended and the other began; harder still to land any blows on the Doberman's body. But suddenly, as if realizing a rescuer was at hand, the smaller dog broke free and ran into the grove of trees. Instead of following, the Doberman turned on Joey.

Joey saw the sharp fangs and the beady, blazing eyes just before the Doberman lunged at him. He jumped to one side and swung the stick hard against the dog's shoulder, where it broke into a dozen pieces. Inspired by fear, Joey leaped at the momentarily confused dog, waving his arms and kicking. He heard a blood curdling yell and realized it was his own. It was as if some wild animal within himself had risen up to meet the challenge. With a snarl, the Doberman slunk off a few feet. When Joey charged again, still shouting as if he meant to tear the dog limb from limb, the Doberman turned tail and ran.

As the rage left him, Joey's legs began to tremble. He saw a trail of blood and quickly followed it into the grove of trees. He saw the smaller dog watching him warily from the far end of the grove. It had short, matted brown hair, the legs of a hound, the head of a collie. Nothing matched; it looked as if it had been put together out of spare parts by a child. Joey went a few steps closer.

"Easy, boy," he called softly. "I won't hurt you. Let's see how badly he sliced you up."

The dog regarded him with deep, watery eyes. Joey called again and the dog's tail wagged once. Finally, as if he had read Joey's intent and found it kind, he trotted over and allowed himself to be patted and stroked.

"It's okay, boy," Joey soothed him. "It's okay, it's okay." He examined the dog, found several bald patches where his fur had been torn out by the Doberman, but only one wound: a three-inch gash across the right rib cage. The blood was already congealing there.

"No problem," Joey said. He scratched the dog's ears. "Did you wander onto that Doberman's turf? He nearly got you."

The dog whined softly. Joey examined his collar. It was old and frayed. There were no tags. The dog was little more than skin drawn loosely over bone.

"Well, nobody owns you, so we'll take you home and get that cut cleaned up. And give you a good meal." Joey took off his belt and looped it through the dog's collar, improvising a leash. The dog barked twice.

"Maybe it's time you had a home," Joey told him. "The streets are no place for a dog like you." Joey laughed. "You have too much class."

The dog trotted along beside him on the makeshift leash as if they had belonged to each other for years. There were a few people on the streets now: early churchgoers, people packing up their cars for a day at the beach. But he was still walking through a city essentially asleep, clinging to its early hours of coolness and quiet.

"The building I live in has a rule about pets," Joey told the dog. "So we have to be quiet going in. Dad will be asleep, so we can get by him all right." Already Joey's mind was racing ahead, trying to figure a way he could keep the dog.

Joey kept talking to the dog as they walked. When the few people they passed turned to stare or smile, Joey ignored them. The need to talk to his new friend was strong, coming from his deep loneliness.

"Who cares what people think?" Joey whispered to the dog. "Do you care?" Joey laughed. "I don't care, either."

The hour of the day was on their side. The Sunday silence gripped his building. The foyer downstairs was empty, as was the elevator going up. The dog didn't seem afraid on the ride.

"You're a real city dog," Joey whispered approvingly.

He unlocked the door and slipped inside with the dog. The drapes were still closed, the room still deep in its artificial dusk. From his father's bedroom came the sound of snoring, steady and rhythmic.

"Quiet now," Joey said softly to the dog. "Not a sound out of you or our goose is cooked before we start."

Joey took the dog into the shower with him and washed him, being particularly thorough over the gash in his side. The dog disliked the water, trembling beneath Joey's firm hands; but he already trusted Joey enough to accept this treatment. After drying him as completely as he could, Joey put antiseptic ointment on the wound and then cleaned up the bathroom.

Outside in the corridor, Joey listened for the snoring from his father's room, then quickly led the dog into his own bedroom. The dog immediately began to explore every corner.

Joey pulled on his jeans and a clean shirt. "Now be quiet while I get you some milk. We'll go out for something better once you're dry."

While Joey was in the kitchen pouring milk into a cereal bowl, the dog started to whine in his room. Joey hurried back with the milk.

"I wasn't gone long," Joey told him.

He put the bowl down. It was empty in no time. While the dog cleaned up the stray drops, Joey went after more, bringing back the whole quart.

"That will have to hold you," he said when that was gone, too. He took a blanket from his closet and made a bed for the dog in the corner by the window, under his desk. With some coaxing, he managed to get the dog to lie down.

"Soon as you're dry, we'll go after something more to eat," Joey repeated. He waited for a moment until he was sure the dog would stay put, then he lay down on his own bed and picked up the book he was reading. The first time he glanced up from the page, the dog was watching him intently; but the next time, the dog was sound asleep.

Joey put down his book. He had never had a dog; he had always wanted one. He already knew in his heart that

33

he would do whatever he had to to keep this new friend.

He remembered the Gypsy girl outside the arcade yesterday. He lay back on his pillow and closed his eyes and tried to remember the verse she had recited. Something about two people or two things coming into his life. Joey struggled to remember the exact words. Something about two, then one would die and the other . . .

He couldn't remember.

He opened his eyes and looked at the dog. Was this dog one of the two who would come into his life? Was he the one who would die, or was he the one who would do the other thing the Gypsy girl had spoken of, the thing he couldn't now remember?

It was probably nonsense. Joey was growing sleepy. He had slept little the night before, out on the balcony. Waves of tiredness now rose up around him like an incoming tide. He saw for a moment a dream vision of the Gypsy girl, saw for the smallest second her lips moving as she recited the verse. He heard the words, all of them, as clearly as if she were saying them to him again; and, for just that fleeting moment before he slept, he understood what they meant.

5

Joey dreamed that his bed collapsed, pinning him under the headboard, and he woke up to find the dog sleeping beside him, his head on Joey's chest. Joey stroked his ears. The dog opened his eyes and looked at him guiltily, but he made no move to get off the bed.

"It's okay," Joey whispered. "I wouldn't want to sleep on a blanket in the corner either." Joey squirmed out from under the dog and sat on the edge of his bed, rubbing his face. The clock on his night table read three. He had slept all morning and half the afternoon.

"Well, boy, I'm really hungry now."

The dog slapped his tail on the bed. Joey studied him. "You don't look half bad, now that you're clean. Next thing we have to do is give you a name."

Joey looked around the room, searching for inspiration. His eyes swept over his bookcase. "That's an idea." He took down one of the books and flipped through it. "Butch Cas-

35

sidy. We'll call you Butch, since you've been living like an outlaw." Joey looked at the dog. "Okay, Butch?"

The dog wagged his tail.

Joey made a leash from an extra belt. They slipped out of the apartment, Joey making sure first that his father was not in the living room.

"He's still sleeping, or else he went out again," Joey told Butch as they waited for the elevator. "Me and Dad . . ." He searched for the right words, then smiled when he remembered he was only talking to a dog. "Well, what do you care about me and Dad?"

They passed Mrs. Murphy in the foyer downstairs. She glared at the dog. Joey nodded and wished her a good day.

"That's all we need," Joey said as they left the building. "Nosy as she is."

They walked several blocks to a Burger King. Joey tied Butch to a post with the belt, then went inside and bought two hamburgers for each of them and a couple of cartons of milk. Butch barked all the time he was inside.

"You're going to have to get over that," Joey scolded him when he came out with the food. "How are we going to hide you if you bark every time I leave?"

Butch squirmed eagerly, waiting for the food, paying no attention to the scolding. Joey unwrapped the hamburgers for him and watched him wolf them down as if there were no prospects of another meal.

"Things were tough for you, weren't they, Butch?" Joey stroked his ears. "Well, it's time for a change." Joey unwrapped his own meal. "For both of us."

That night Joey heard his father moving through the apartment, taking a shower, rattling things in the kitchen.

"You hungry, Joey?" he called.

Joey looked at Butch. "No, I already ate."

His father didn't insist, and later Joey heard the television go on.

"We can do this," Joey whispered to Butch. "He won't even know you're here." But for Joey it was more of a prayer than a certainty.

His father stayed up late, and Butch had been pacing the room for an hour before Joey was finally able to sneak him outside for a walk. As they wandered together through the dark, quiet streets, thunder rumbled from a storm to the west, and the sky overhead reflected the city's lights in glowing red.

They were back inside before the storm hit the city, and in his room Joey sat in the dark and watched the lightning flashes through his window.

"Tough night for anyone stuck outside," he whispered to the dog.

Butch was trembling after each crash of thunder, as if remembering other storms when he had had no safe haven. They fell asleep as the storm slowly rumbled off to the east, with Joey lying there beside the dog, whispering to him not to be afraid.

By the time they were up Monday morning, Joey's father had gone to work. They sat on the balcony and ate a large breakfast of pancakes and bacon.

"That's all," Joey said as the dog crunched up the last piece of bacon. "You know, soon as you're up to a decent weight you're going to have to get used to one meal a day. Otherwise you'll get so fat the next Doberman you meet will gobble you up before you can run a block."

37

The storm had brought in cooler air, and Joey could see parts of Boston that had been hidden in the haze for a week. They spent the morning on the balcony. The habit of talking to the dog was so ingrained by now that Joey was hardly conscious of it. He told the dog about Betty, and Butch kept cocking his head as if he wished he could understand.

"She would like you a lot, Butch," Joey said. "And Mom would have liked you too if she'd lived long enough to meet you. She was killed on Boston Common when she tried to grab her purse back from a couple of muggers. They hit her with a piece of pipe. Half a dozen people saw it happen. They didn't even try to help her."

Butch yelped. Joey realized he was squeezing the dog's neck with his hand. "Sorry. I still get . . . " Joey pulled his hand away and wiped the sweat off on his jeans.

"I miss her, you know? And Dad's changed so much since she died, it's like I've lost him, too." Scenes from the past flashed through Joey's mind like fragments from a movie cut with scissors and patched together out of sequence: his father at the graveside, talking to no one; the flowers that had filled the room where his mother's coffin rested during the service before the long ride out to the cemetery; the grief-stricken voice of Granddad Webster when they talked to each other on the telephone the day his mother had died. . . .

Tears were streaming down his face. He wiped them away with his fingers. Through a blur he saw the dog looking at him.

"I don't usually cry anymore," he said. "So don't worry, I'm not gloomy like Dad. Besides, we're getting out of here soon. You'll like Vermont. My grandparents live on a lake where the trees come right down to the water's edge and you'll have all kinds of animals to chase."

Joey gathered up the dishes and took them into the kitchen to wash. Butch followed him, his toenails clicking on the tiles. "And you'll love Granddad Webster," Joey said. "He's patient and kind, and he knows how you feel even without asking you."

Another picture flashed through Joey's mind, of his grandfather going for a walk with him after his mother's funeral, not saying a word about her, just talking about little things; and yet both of them knowing that they were sharing her memory more deeply than words could express.

Joey scrubbed hard on the dishes. "Tell you what, Butch. Soon as I get done here, we'll go for a run along the river."

The rest of the day passed with the feeling of a dream. They ran along the Charles River and afterwards bought hot dogs and sat beside the water, watching the rowing crews glide by in their shells. Great puffy white clouds drifted by on the clean northwest wind, and the grass smelled sweet from last night's rain.

Joey roused himself at last and headed back toward the apartment.

"Got to get you in before Dad comes home," he told Butch, who trotted along at his side. "And you're going to be quiet while I eat supper. Understand?"

They reached the apartment without being seen. By the time Joey's father came home from work, Butch was asleep in Joey's room and Joey was cooking spaghetti for supper. With the air conditioner off, they ate out on the balcony.

"What did you do today?" his father asked from behind his newspaper.

"Ran by the river."

His father poured the rest of his beer into his glass and looked over at him. "What did you put in this sauce?"

Joey shrugged. "Some spices."

His father grunted. "I guess. It could burn a hole through the roof of your mouth." His father separated a meatball from the sauce and speared it with his fork. From down on the street below the traffic sounds floated up to them. The sky above Boston was a luminous, evening blue.

"And what smells so strong around here?" his father asked. "Are you taking your showers?"

Joey nodded. "Sure I am."

"You don't always."

"Could be a musty smell left over from the hot weather."

"Smells like a dog."

Joey laughed. "Maybe one of the neighbors is breaking the rules."

"What's that?" his father demanded.

Joey shook his head, but his heart was sinking. Butch was scratching on the bedroom door. While they sat listening, he started to bark.

"What the hell is going on here?"

"Sounds like a dog," Joey said.

"I know it sounds like a dog." His father stood up and walked into the living room. Joey tried to head him off, but they both reached his room at the same time. His father opened the door and Butch lunged out, jumping eagerly around Joey's legs.

"Damn it, Joey, when are you going to grow up?"

Butch kept barking and pulling at the cuffs of his jeans. The more Joey tried to quiet him, the more excited he became.

"Joey, you . . ." The telephone rang and his father went to answer it.

"Hello? Yes, Mrs. Murphy, I know it's a dog. No, Mrs. Murphy, I'm well aware of the rules in this building. Yes, I see. Well, it's not staying, I can assure you of that."

40

His father slammed down the receiver and glared at him. "Tomorrow, Joey. Take that dog to the animal shelter. Don't let me find it here tomorrow night."

Joey glared back at him but said nothing. He found the leash and took Butch out for a walk.

6

In the gray light of Tuesday morning Joey woke up to the sounds of his father fixing his own breakfast. Butch was sleeping beside him on the bed.

"I'm not giving you up," Joey whispered. He had slept badly, pursued by a nightmare Doberman who was after both of them, who had chased them through empty city streets where every door was locked. "We'll leave," Joey whispered. "We'll hike up to Vermont. We don't have time now to wait for an invitation."

Butch thumped his tail on the bed.

His father poked his head in before he left for work. He stared at the dog on Joey's bed.

"Are you ever going to grow up?" he asked.

"You asked me that last night."

"Yes, and you didn't answer it then, either."

"Is there some special age when I'm not supposed to like dogs anymore?"

42

His father studied him. "The dog goes, Joey. Before I get home tonight."

When he was gone, the door clicking behind him, Joey vaulted into his jeans, and made a quick breakfast. "To hell with him," he said to Butch. "We'll send him a postcard someday that'll say, 'Having a wonderful time, glad you're not here.' "

Joey laughed and repeated the joke softly to himself.

After breakfast he climbed into his closet and found his backpack and sleeping bag. He hadn't used them since an outing with the hiking club at school over a year ago. While the bag was airing on the balcony railing, he went through his pack, making sure he had the minimum of things he would need to camp out on the way north.

There was only forty-two dollars left in his stash. He counted it twice, hoping there was more. It had to last them all the way to his grandparents' house in Carverville, Vermont. Rummaging through his father's desk, he found maps of the New England states and selected one for New Hampshire and one for Vermont. Spreading them out on the living-room floor, he traced several possible routes. They would have to stay off highways, keep to the secondary roads, attract as little attention to themselves as possible.

"We don't want the cops picking us up," he said, scratching Butch's ears. "We want to look like we know just what we're doing and where we're going."

On an impulse he also took a map for Massachusetts. It didn't make any sense to get lost leaving Boston.

He interrupted his packing to take Butch for a quick walk. When he got back, he cut a length of rope from a coil in his backpack and fashioned a longer leash for the dog.

"How's this?" he asked, trying it on the dog. "Soon as we get into real country, I'll let you run loose."

He searched the kitchen cupboards for food they could take that would be easy to prepare. As he was filling his canteen, the telephone rang.

His first impulse was to let it ring. Then he thought that Granddad Webster might have received his letter, and he hurried to answer it.

"Hello?"

"Hello, Joey."

It was Betty. Behind her voice he could hear the sounds from her office.

"I tried to call you yesterday," she said. "There was no answer."

"I was out most of the afternoon."

"How are you, Joey? Are you getting along all right?"

"Yeah." Joey wanted to tell her of his plans to leave, but he didn't dare. She might feel it was her duty to call his father. But it was hard for him to lie to her. He was glad he wasn't within reach of her eyes, with her glasses on or off.

"You sure?" Her voice was soft and husky.

"Yeah, sure, Betty. I'm fine."

"And your father?"

"Oh, you know Dad. He doesn't show his feelings much."

"I know."

"I don't think he even has any." Joey tried to swallow down the rage that was suddenly choking him. "Except being angry. That's his one and only feeling, so he uses it all the time."

"Joey?"

He took a deep breath. "Yeah?"

"What's wrong?"

"Nothing."

"You sound upset."

"I'm not." He looked around when Butch barked. The dog

44

was still wearing the rope leash and had tangled himself around a chair.

"What's that?"

"My dog."

"When did . . . "

"I found him." Suddenly Joey understood why Betty had called. "You'd come back if he asked you, wouldn't you?"

The line was silent for a long while. He could hear the whisper of other calls. "Maybe," she said at last.

"He won't ask you, you know." Joey realized how cruel this sounded, but he was too angry to stop himself. "I mean, there's no way he can admit he needs anyone."

"I know."

"So you're lucky to be rid of us."

"I don't feel lucky."

"Well, you should."

"You sound very bitter, Joey."

Joey said nothing.

"I did want to call and find out how you were doing, Joey."

He could barely hear her. "I'm all right," he repeated. "Got it all worked out."

"What?"

"Things."

Butch was still barking. Joey tried to quiet him.

"Glad you have a dog, Joey," Betty said. "Good-bye."

He held the receiver for a moment longer, his own good-bye already too late for her to hear. Then he hung up.

"It's you and me, Butch," he said as he untangled the dog. "Just you and me."

Before he left he took a picture of his mother from the shelf of photographs in the living room and tucked it safely into his backpack. For a second he wondered whether to leave a note for his father, but there was nothing he could think to say.

He shouldered the pack with the sleeping bag slung beneath it on the frame. "Come on, Butch. Let's go." He grabbed the dog's rope leash and walked out the door, with one last look back at the empty apartment.

Part Two
THE ROAD

7

The road baked under the noon sun, within a silence so thick it seemed like deafness. Joey felt the weight of his backpack grow heavier with each step. Butch trotted beside him at the sandy edge of the road, his tongue hanging out. He was no longer interested in running after rabbits or treeing squirrels.

When Joey looked back, he saw the road through a shimmer of heat: a wide gray line slipping over the low hills they had been crossing since breaking camp this morning. There was little traffic. No one had stopped to give them a ride.

Yesterday, his first day on the road, he had caught several rides, the last one bringing him into New Hampshire. He and the dog had camped in a hollow some distance from the road, near a trickle of a stream. During the night the hot weather had returned on a south wind, and now summer smoked around them as they walked.

Butch trotted ahead to a patch of shade beneath a clump of low pines and sat down. He looked back as Joey plodded toward him as if to beg for a lunch break, an afternoon nap, a frolic in the woods, anything that would mean an end to their long walk beneath the summer sun.

"Not here," Joey told him. "Let's find a place out of sight of the road."

Joey looked back. He felt uneasy, as if the police might come along at any minute to ask questions he wouldn't be able to answer. This anxiety had followed him yesterday out of Boston and grown stronger with each mile on their way north. They were keeping to back roads, avoiding towns as much as possible, even at the risk of getting lost.

"Someone's coming." Joey stared through the heat waves. Slowly, soundlessly, a car was cresting one of the hills behind them. Joey waited impatiently for it to reappear on the nearer ridge. "It's okay," he said at last. "It's an old car. Not the cops."

Butch reached out and scratched one of Joey's legs with his paw. Joey looked down.

"Let's wait. Maybe we can get a ride. Maybe it's a farmer who would like some company, and you can ride with your face out the window and smell the wind." It felt real to Joey as he described it, as if they were already gliding over the road, laughing at their past discomfort.

"God, it's slow," Joey said later when the car was again out of sight. Finally it topped the last hill and rolled down into the valley between them.

Joey could see it more clearly now: an old Ford from the early fifties, maybe black under all that dust, rusty, battered, barely moving. It backfired twice, drifted onto the shoulder of the road, and stopped in the very hollow of the valley he and Butch had just spent what seemed like hours climbing out of, at least a mile back the way they had come.

50

Joey shook his head. "It didn't even make it. It didn't even get as far as here." He watched a moment or two longer, waiting to see someone get out and lift the car's hood. When no one did, he began to wonder what was wrong. He looked down at Butch, then into the woods where the cool shade beckoned.

"Come on, Butch," he said at last with a weary sigh. "We can't go off and leave them there to bake in the heat."

The dog barked in protest. Joey bent down and patted his side. "I know. We're going the wrong way."

As if to tempt them one last time, a breeze drifted from the woods, carrying the smells of cool, green shade, a hidden brook, and the last drops of the dewy morning. He hesitated. Then he turned regretfully away and began walking toward the car. Behind him, Butch followed with his head down, his tongue nearly dragging on the ground.

The windshield was so discolored that Joey did not see the woman slumped over the steering wheel until he was close to the car. He broke into a jog despite the weight of his pack and covered the last yards in seconds.

"Are you okay?" he asked. When the woman didn't answer, he forced himself to open the door and touch her arm. Her skin felt hot and dry under his fingers. Gently he eased her back against the seat. Her eyelids fluttered.

"Are you sick? Do you need help?"

She was a thin woman with brown, leathery, sunburned skin. Her long, dark hair, almost black except where it was streaked with white, was pulled back and tied behind her head. Her age was hard to guess. It might have been forty-five, it might have been sixty. Despite her thinness and the confused look on her face as she slowly came out of her faint, she looked like someone who had spent years outdoors, someone who knew how to take care of herself.

"What did I do?" she demanded in a surprisingly deep voice, a rich tenor that came from a body that looked too small to produce it. "Did I faint?"

Joey nodded. "I think you did."

Her eyes were deep-set and brown, with flakes of gold fire in them as she stared at him. "And who are you?"

"I'm Joey Carr. That's Butch. We were up the road and saw you stop."

The woman nodded. "I remember what happened now. I think I'm out of gas." She tried to restart the car, but it only growled unproductively. She switched off the key. "The gauge is off. Damn that Tod." She turned back toward Joey and stuck out her hand. "I'm Hannah Adams."

Her fingers wrapped around his; the grip was strong and firm. As he helped her out of the car, he was struck immediately by the paradox of this woman: She seemed so strong for someone so weak. She could barely stand; her body was swaying as if at any moment she might keel over again. Yet under all this was something hard and tough, as if a spirit inside her struggled to free itself from the weakness of the flesh. Her legs buckled as Joey helped her off the road, but her voice was imperious and sure when she pointed to a lone tree in the field near them.

"Take me over there," she said. "I'll sit in the shade awhile, and then I'll go after gas."

"I'll go," Joey said as he eased her down onto the grass beneath the tree. "The last station we saw was back a good five miles."

Hannah Adams studied him as he swung off his pack and retrieved his canteen. He poured some water onto his handkerchief and handed it to her.

52

"Tell me, Joey Carr," she said as she bathed her face with the damp handkerchief, "why do you bother to help me?"

Joey shrugged. "No reason." He poured out a cup of water for Butch, then took a drink himself.

He realized Hannah was grinning at him. "I like you, Joey," she said. "So I guess I'll let you help me."

He found an empty gallon can in the trunk, under the rubble of spare tires and odd wheels. Before he left, Hannah made him crank up the windows of the car and lock the doors. The back seat was piled high with boxes and old, black suitcases.

"And bring me my bag," she called. "The one on the front seat."

He reopened the car and found the bag: a large sack of soft brown leather with a drawstring at the top. When he picked it up, he was surprised at its weight.

"What's in it?" he asked as he dropped it beside her in the shade.

She ignored his question and handed him two dollars. "For the gas."

"Are you sure that's the problem?" Joey asked.

"No, but I haven't filled the tank since early yesterday, and I've come a long way. I know the gauge is off. It's been off all the way from New Jersey. But it's totally bonkers today."

She shrugged and smiled up at him. "Damn that Tod. He never warned me. I do think it's the gas, Joey."

"Okay," he agreed. "I should be back in three hours at the most. I'll leave my water and backpack here, and Butch can keep you company."

The dog was already lying with his head in Hannah's lap, but he got to his feet and started to follow as Joey walked to the road with the gas can.

"No, Butch, you stay here. Stay!"

When Joey reached the top of the first hill, he looked back and saw Butch sitting with Hannah under the lonely tree in the field. They made a strange pair in that small circle of shade, framed as they were by the shimmering heat waves, dwarfed by the blazing sky above them. He waved once, then turned to continue on his way.

8

It was a long walk to the gas station. The anxiety he had felt earlier in the day returned, worse now that he was retracing his steps. He wasn't feeling guilty about leaving his father, but he could not feel sure that he and Butch would ever reach his grandparents' house in Carverville, Vermont.

The gas station occupied a forgotten crossroads at the edge of a small town.

"Ran her dry, eh, boy?" the old man working the pumps asked him.

Joey nodded.

"Hot day for a walk."

"Yeah."

"Remember to save a little to put into the carburetor." The old man handed him the filled can. "Don't pour it all into the tank."

Joey nodded. "Thank you."

He had enough money left after paying for the gas to buy a

bottle of Coke. He did not open it. The bag ripped before he had gone a mile, so he took off his shirt to make a sling and carried the bottle that way.

The air grew hotter as the afternoon crawled slowly by. He shifted his burdens from one arm to the other, but this did not help his aching feet. A cloud of gas fumes wafted up into his face from the loose cap on the can. His stomach churned with nausea.

Butch met him a mile from the car. Joey put down the gas and the bottle of Coke and hugged him. "You were supposed to wait with Mrs. Adams."

Butch pulled free and darted around his legs. "You're a nut," Joey said with a grin as he tried to pat him. "I see the long siesta did you a world of good."

Butch barked. Joey picked up the sling and the gas can and hurried toward the car. He wondered if the woman had fainted again.

But Hannah was sitting as before under the tree, and she looked up and waved to him as soon as he came into sight. She was reading when he joined her in the shade beneath the tree. She put away the book and smiled at him. Her deep brown eyes flashed fire as they looked into his.

"Well, Joey, I owe you a return favor now."

Joey shrugged. He gave her the bottle of Coke, which was warm by now. It foamed over when he opened it for her. She drank a little and then handed it back to him. Joey hefted the canteen and was surprised to find it still nearly full.

"Your dog found a puddle of water, and my needs are very little now," Hannah told him. She reached over and stroked the dog. "He's a good companion for you, Joey. He wanted to obey you, and he did for a very long time, but then he simply had to go after you." She looked up. "So I let him."

Again Joey sensed something strange about the woman, something rock-hard and wise that peered out at him through her flashing eyes. He broke away and took the gas can to the car.

Remembering what the old man at the gas station had told him, Joey poured all but a little of the gas into the car's tank, then lifted the hood, took off the air filter and poured a few drops down the throat of the carburetor. He fetched the keys from Hannah and sat behind the wheel.

The air in the car was like that in an overheated attic—it burned his throat and filled his nostrils with the smell of old clothes. He shook his head and tried the starter.

The engine caught and died. He got out, dribbled more gas into the carburetor, and tried again. This time the engine started, held through a series of coughs and sputters, then smoothed out. He ran it for a moment longer, then switched it off.

"It *was* the gas, Mrs. Adams," he called as he got out.

"That's a blessing," she answered.

By the time he opened the car's windows, she had walked over from the tree with his backpack.

"You shouldn't have bothered with that, Mrs. Adams," he said. "It's too heavy."

Her eyes snapped fire as she looked at him now without smiling. "First of all, young man, I'm not Mrs. Adams, I'm Miss Adams, and anyone I care about had better call me Hannah. Secondly, although I occasionally do accept favors, I always return them. And I never, never accept charity or condescension." As if to emphasize her point, she lifted his backpack and shoved it into the back of the car among all her boxes and suitcases.

Joey tried to hide his confusion by replacing the air filter and closing the hood. "I thought you were sick," he said at last.

She nodded. "I am. I'm dying. But until then, I'll carry my share of the load." Her deep voice dropped a tone lower as she touched his shoulder with her dry, leathery hand. "It's the only way we can travel together, Joey."

He looked at her.

"Well, you didn't think I was going to drive off and leave you here"—she waved one hand at the field shimmering in the afternoon sunlight—"here in this forsaken place, did you?"

When room had been made for Butch in the back, they both got into the front and Hannah started the engine. She nodded with satisfaction.

"The first thing, Joey, is to drive to the next town and fill this thing up with gas." She looked over at him. "Then we'll be on our way. I don't know where you're going yet, but I have an idea it's a good distance. If you can be patient while I visit a few places I've a mind to visit, I'll see that you get where you're going to. Fair enough?"

He nodded. Hannah put the car into gear and they lurched ahead. Butch barked and put his head out the window and sniffed the air blowing by.

A few miles along the road they pulled into a town, where they bought gas and a bag of fruit at a small village store. Joey ate two oranges as they drove out into the country again. He could only persuade Hannah to eat one small piece.

"Food doesn't agree with me much anymore," she told him. "Sometimes I forget to eat, it bothers me so. That's probably why I fainted today." She motioned toward the glove compartment. "Get out one of those maps and see if you can figure out where we are."

Joey bent over the map for several minutes. "I think we're somewhere northwest of Nashua."

"That narrows it down a whole lot."

Joey grinned. "I didn't notice the name of that town where we stopped."

"Neither did I. These back roads are like a maze." Hannah forced the car to go fast enough for her to shift it into third. "What I'm looking for is any road heading toward Clarkburg Corners."

As they drove, Joey told her a little about why he was on the road. She was able to guess much that he didn't tell her.

"There's a time for running away in everyone's life," she said. She turned to look at him for a moment. "It makes a difference, though, whether you're running toward something or away from something."

Joey was silent.

"You know in your heart which it is for you."

Butch stuck his head over the seat and licked Joey's ear.

"I suppose you're curious about who I am and what I'm about," Hannah went on.

Joey nodded.

"Well, curiosity is a healthy thing. Keeps us young, keeps us going. And since I trust you, Joey, I'll tell you the truth. I'm considered a witch by many who know me, and that's not far off. And what I'm looking for is something the doctors back home in New Jersey couldn't give me."

Joey stared at her. "What's that?"

"Life, Joey. All they have back there for me is death."

The afternoon was drawing long shadows across the road when they came to the first signboard for Clarkburg Corners. They turned onto a wide, gravel road heading west. The sun blazed before them as it sank toward the far hills, and on both sides the woods came in more closely. At the next fork in the road, Hannah chose the narrower way, and they bounced then over hard ruts as the branches of trees scraped the car.

"It's here close by," Hannah said several times. "There are things I recognize."

The road climbed a washboard hill. At the top, an overgrown meadow opened up on the right, and the sun struck the windows of an abandoned farmhouse. Hannah stopped the car at the edge of the driveway that had once connected the road to the barn. Above them the derelict house glowed red in the rays of the setting sun.

"Here we are," Hannah said.

"Where?" Joey asked.

"Home, or what used to be my home, years ago."

They both got out, and Butch raced off to chase a woodchuck he had spotted on a knoll in the meadow. His barking gave a frantic edge to the silence that engulfed the old farm.

"I'm going to look around," Hannah told him. "I won't be long."

As she climbed rickety steps to the side porch, Joey looked up at the house. For just a second he thought he saw a movement in one window, the fleeting image of a face behind the shattered panes of glass. Then it was gone. It might only have been a torn window shade blowing in the wind, except that right now, at sunset, the air was deathly still.

9

Down in the meadow Butch was circling the knoll where the woodchuck had been sighted. His barks echoed from the wall of trees beyond. Joey went down into the grass after him.

"He's long gone, Butch," Joey told the dog. Butch was thrusting his nose into every depression in the ground, snorting loudly. Joey laughed and sat on the top of the knoll. The sun had dipped below the distant hills, and the sky now was shaded with variations of its light.

Joey watched the house. It brooded above the meadow, its gaunt windows with their shards of glass bearing mute testimony to the ruin within. The hush of evening was upon the day, yet here there was a silence even deeper, a sense of time gone by and lost forever.

Butch trotted up the knoll and stuck his wet nose under Joey's arm. "What do you think, Butch?" Joey asked. "She says she's a witch." He scratched the dog's ears. "I don't

61

know if I believe that, but there is something strange about her."

They left the knoll and walked to the barn and explored the dark, stone rooms of its lowest floor. Joey found several treasures, including a broken powder horn, but he felt compelled to leave everything where he found it. He laughed nervously. This was the sort of place that made you superstitious against your own best judgment. When Butch knocked over a pile of boxes, Joey spun around to face him. He realized he was holding his breath.

"Let's go," Joey said. He led the way outside, around to the front. He called Hannah's name. When there was no answer, he climbed up onto the porch. Butch began to growl.

"Be quiet." He thought he heard voices coming from somewhere within the house. Inside the first room, his feet crunched on fallen plaster. When Butch growled again, Joey looked down and saw that the hair was standing up on the back of the dog's neck.

He patted Butch and continued on into a hallway. The only light came in through the broken front door, from the evening glow outside. Now he could distinctly hear two voices, Hannah's and one pitched much higher than hers: a squeaky voice that sent shivers down his spine. Both voices were raised in argument, yet he could not make out what they were saying.

"Hannah?" he called again, but her name came out as a whisper. When he started up the stairs, Butch began to whine urgently and would not follow. Joey went on without him.

Upstairs, there was more light. The hallway ran by three rooms, all with open doors. There were no voices now, only a silence thick with dust. The first two rooms were empty except for bedframes, and in one, the ruin of a mattress. In the third bedroom he found Hannah sitting by a window that looked out upon the meadow.

As he entered the room, he felt something cold brush his arm, slipping past him as he came in. Yet all he saw were cobwebs, hanging from the ceiling in twists of dusty gray.

"Hannah?"

She turned toward him. She was crying silently; he could see tears on the side of her face that was illuminated by light from the window.

"I thought I heard you talking with someone," he said.

She stood up. "It's late, Joey. Let's find a place for the night. We can't stay here."

She led the way downstairs, to where Butch eagerly awaited them. To Joey's taut senses, it seemed as if someone else followed them, down the stairs and out through the kitchen to the side porch. He tried to ask Hannah about it, but she silenced him with a shake of her head.

"Not now, Joey. We have to leave."

They drove back to where the road had last forked and found a place to pull the car into the bushes above a small stream. While Hannah built a fire, Joey cleared the campsite and gathered dry wood. It was completely dark by the time he unpacked two cans of stew and poured them into a pot to heat over the flames. While they waited, they munched on the last of the fruit they had bought earlier.

"You're very quiet, Joey," Hannah said at last.

"I'm confused," he admitted.

"About what?"

"About you."

"Would you rather we went our separate ways?"

He shook his head. "No." He looked at her in the firelight.

The night about them fluttered with a thousand insects. "I like you. It feels good being with you. You're not..." He searched for the right words. "You're not like other older people I've known."

She laughed. "But?"

He plunged ahead. "Are you really a witch?"

"Ah, the voice of doubt."

"I don't mean I think you're lying."

"You just can't quite believe in me?"

He shrugged. "Before I left Boston, a Gypsy girl told me I would meet two. She didn't say two what. The next day I rescued Butch from a Doberman, and now I've met you."

"Most Gypsies are frauds," Hannah said.

"This one was different. She seemed as surprised at what she told me as I was." He stirred the stew as it began to steam. "There's some bread in my pack."

Hannah pulled out the bread, which was badly flattened but still edible. He dished out the stew, leaving some in the pot to cool for Butch. While they ate, Hannah looked across at him. She finished before him, leaving half her stew uneaten.

"You should eat more," he told her.

She shook her head.

After he had washed the dishes in the stream, he returned to the fire with more wood. The night seemed full of hidden eyes, but he knew it was only his imagination.

"Well, Joey," Hannah said softly, "I can't prove to you that I'm a witch if you don't believe. I won't even try. That's not the point of belief. It's something you have to work out for yourself. All I can tell you is that I would not on purpose try to confuse or bewilder you."

Her thin face was a flicker of lines and shadows cast by the firelight. She looked much older tonight; her voice was low.

64

"Back at that house," Joey began. "I felt like . . ."

"Don't try to pin everything down with words," Hannah told him. "If you experienced something there, it's sufficient just to know that."

"But I want to understand."

"Everything?"

Joey hesitated. "Yes."

Hannah laughed softly. She got up from her resting place against his backpack and reached over to her leather bag. She opened the drawstring and began rummaging inside.

"Look into the fire," she told him. "Think about something you'd like to know, then tell me what it is."

He studied the curling flames as they etched their way over the wood. His heart was beating strangely, hard and fast. Suddenly Hannah was there beside him.

"Tell me what you'd like to know," she whispered.

"About my father. I'd like to know what he's doing tonight. How he feels, now that I'm gone."

Her hand darted by, tossing a cloud of powder into the flames. For a moment the fire seemed to expand, to stretch into sheets of yellow like burning panes of glass. Then the flames exploded, sending firebrands all about the camp. Butch howled and bolted for the woods. Joey slapped wildly at his smoldering jeans.

Hannah was cursing beside him as she beat at her own clothes. Together they raced around the camp putting out the fires that had started on all sides.

"I should know better," Hannah growled. "Damn me anyway! That's what I get for trying magic with an unbeliever."

Later, when order had been restored to their camp, Butch slunk back from the woods and settled down beside Joey.

From time to time he glanced over at Hannah with an aggrieved tilt to his head, as if to ask her why she had disrupted things so. At last he put his head down on his paws and closed his eyes.

Joey was the one to break the silence. "You said that old farmhouse was your home?"

"Yes. I lived there when I was little, with my maiden aunt Polly, after my parents died. She raised me until I was sixteen." Hannah paused. "Those weren't happy years. After that, I went to live with my cousin Tod and his wife in New Jersey, went to college, then taught school at the Winslow Academy for Girls."

"Is that Tod's car?" Joey asked, remembering how she had cursed his name earlier when she had run out of gas.

She nodded. "He sold it to me for three hundred dollars."

Joey didn't say anything.

"He cheated me, I guess."

"Maybe not."

"He promised me it would take me as far as I wanted to go."

"How far are you going?"

"Where did you say your grandparents live?"

"Carverville, Vermont. It's up in the Northeast Kingdom."

"Then I'm going at least as far as Carverville, Vermont."

Hannah arranged a place for herself in the car to sleep. Joey unrolled his sleeping bag beside the fire. But he could not sleep, and as the fire died, he watched the stars revolving slowly above the trees. He decided at last that if Hannah was a witch, she wasn't a very good one.

But maybe she was right. Maybe his doubts had spoiled her spell and set their camp on fire.

10

Hannah was already dressed when he woke up the next morning. Her long, brightly printed skirt swept the ground as she gathered up the cooking gear and put it away in his backpack. Her vitality had returned and her eyes again flashed with their inner fire as she teased him about his laziness. Silver earrings dangled from each side of her head, and a heavy silver necklace hung around her neck.

"Let's go, Joey, while it's still cool."

When she wasn't looking, he climbed out of his sleeping bag and into his jeans. There were patches of ground fog down by the stream, but overhead the sky was clear. When he walked down to the stream to wash, Butch followed him and waded into the shallow water.

"Great," Joey told him. "You have to ride in a car, you know."

Butch poked his nose into the water, then shook himself and sneezed.

"Come on, get out of there."

Back at the camp, Joey tried to dry himself with his one towel, made a face and finished drying with his shirt. "I'm going to need a laundromat soon," he said.

Hannah was delving into her leather bag. "We'll buy some cold-water soap and find a stream tonight where we can wash out what we need."

"What's in that bag, anyway?"

Hannah pulled on the drawstring and looked up. "If I told you, you wouldn't believe me."

"Try me."

She shook her head. "Make sure the fire's out. We'll find a place for breakfast. My treat."

They stopped in the next town to eat. Joey worked his way through two orders of pancakes, while Hannah settled for toast and coffee. Joey watched her, but said nothing. With his own money he bought a carton of milk for Butch.

By ten o'clock they were crossing the congested central corridor of the state, which runs along both sides of Route 93. Avoiding Manchester, they pushed on past Concord toward the lakes. Joey had the map on his lap to keep track of their progress. Hannah seemed to know where she was going, and as long as the way led generally north, Joey had no objection to the zigzags of their progress.

Below Lake Winnipesaukee, the engine began to rap loudly. They stopped while Joey checked the oil.

"There's nothing on the dipstick," he told Hannah. They drove to the next gas station and put in three quarts. As they continued on, Joey listened closely to the engine and heard the rap again, less obvious now but still there. He exchanged a look with Hannah.

"Damn that Tod," she said. "Damn him all to . . ."

"Watch out!"

Hannah swerved to avoid the truck that had pulled across their path from a side road. For the next hour she was intent on the heavy traffic around the lakes; but shortly after noon, they found a little lakeside town, neglected for some reason by the throngs of tourists, and bought a picnic lunch in a small market. They walked out onto a pier to eat in the cool air above the water.

"My grandparents live by a lake," Joey said between bites of bologna. "A lot smaller than this one." He looked down at the litter floating by. "A lot cleaner, too."

Hannah studied her sandwich, then drank from the cup of coffee she had bought. "Listen, Joey, I hope you don't mind these side trips we'll be making."

He shook his head. "No problem. That's what I agreed to." He gave Butch a piece of his second sandwich. "I'm in no hurry."

"Good." She looked at him, then out over the water. Her eyes squinted against the glare as a fitful breeze fluttered her long hair, which had come loose behind her head. "I need to make you agree to one other condition."

Something in her voice made Joey stop eating. "What?"

"No matter what happens, Joey, promise me there will be no doctors."

"I don't understand."

She moved closer on the dock and touched his knee. "I have cancer, Joey. The doctors had one go at me and left me worse off than before. Now it's back, and they don't give me much time. That's the one thing I agree with them on. So all the more reason I can't waste any more time on them. I have to look elsewhere."

His eyes were locked onto hers. "What are you looking for?"

She continued to stare at him. Her eyes seemed to glow with a light all their own, a light from deep inside. "Just promise me, Joey. No doctors, no matter what happens to me."

He looked quickly away as he felt tears come into his eyes without warning.

"Ah, Joey, you have a good soul. I'd not ask this of you if I had any other choice. But you must promise me."

He nodded slowly.

"Fine, then. Enough of this gloomy talk." Hannah laughed and patted his knee. "Let's have a start on that chocolate bar before Butch eats it, wrapper and all."

As they drove up into the mountains north of the lakes, Hannah entertained him with stories from her years of teaching at the Winslow Academy for Girls. The miles slipped happily by as she wove a spell with her words. They were able to leave their sadness behind them at the lake, and even forget for a while the persistent rap in the engine that adding oil had only muffled.

In the middle of the afternoon they drove into a small village squeezed up against a ridge of high spruce trees, which loomed dark into the blue mountain sky. Hannah parked the car in front of a small shop beside a sign that read:

AUNT MADDY'S
Jams & Jellies
Rare Herbs & Spices
Country Condiments
&
Diverse Ingredients

70

The shop occupied the front of an old Cape, with an ell that led to a barn at one side. Not a person was astir in the village. A country stupor hung in the air above the street and smothered the few houses that lined it on each side.

Hannah shut off the engine. "You can come in if you'd like," she said. "But Butch had better remain outside."

The front room of the shop was lined with shelves sagging under the weight of hundreds of jam jars. Racks along one wall held bins of spices and dried herbs. Behind a counter, a wrinkled woman who looked at least eighty read a newspaper, paying no attention to them.

Hannah walked over and introduced herself. The crone looked up and studied first Hannah, then Joey, then Hannah again.

"And what might you be after?" she asked in a voice like crinkling paper.

Hannah said something Joey couldn't hear. The old woman cupped her ear. "What say?"

Hannah did not repeat herself, or if she did, she spoke more softly than before. But understanding spread across the old woman's wrinkled face. She nodded with a curious bob of her head.

"Then you'll be wanting to come into the back," she said to Hannah. She looked suspiciously at Joey. "The boy stays out here."

Hannah glanced at Joey before following the ancient shopkeeper through a doorway into the rear of the building. Joey had a momentary glimpse of other shelves there, with rows of large jars containing dried branches and leaves, some with earth-colored powders. Then the door closed.

Joey wandered slowly around the shop, past the shelves of jams and preserves, idly reading their contents. Most of them were made from fruits he'd never heard of, curious

71

names with old-fashioned spellings on the hand-printed labels. Flies ricochetted off the pressed-tin ceiling overhead, their buzzing giving a dry edge to the sultry afternoon. From the back room he could hear nothing.

At least fifteen or twenty minutes drifted by. Joey was nearly asleep on his feet. Then, simultaneously, two sounds shattered the silence: Butch's frantic barking and a chilling scream so high-pitched it made Joey's head hurt.

Both noises came from the back of the building. Joey ran out the door and around the side of the house. A field stretched away from the back lawn. Between the neat, orderly plots of herbs, Butch raced in pursuit of an orange cat, and the old woman followed in pursuit of Butch.

"Joey, don't!" Hannah shouted, but he didn't stop. As Butch angled to the right to cut off the cat's mad dash for some distant trees, he was slowed down by the plants he plowed through. Joey reached him before the old woman did and grabbed his collar. He had just time enough to pull Butch up from the ruin of the plants before the old woman descended upon him with a screech and clawed his face. He ducked away as her nails cut into him.

Through her incoherent screams he tried to apologize for what Butch had done. Backing quickly away from her continued efforts to scratch out his eyes, he stumbled through another plot of herbs, realized the futility of his excuses and turned and ran toward the car, Butch still squirming in his arms.

He put Butch into the back of the car and then stood there trying to bawl the dog out and catch his breath at the same time. When Hannah came out of the shop carrying a small package, he didn't have the courage to meet her eyes.

They hadn't driven more than a hundred yards when

suddenly Hannah stopped the car and collapsed in laughter over the steering wheel. Joey watched her first with concern, then with growing relief as he realized she wasn't angry with him.

"Oh, Joey," she gasped at last, her body still shaking. "You and that dog surely did liven up her afternoon. I wish..." Hannah rocked again with laughter. "I wish you could have seen the view of it I had. The cat and Butch and you and Aunt Maddy...." Hannah sat up straight and wiped her eyes. "I needed that, Joey. But I shouldn't treat it so lightly."

Joey fingered his scratched face. "She nearly tore my eyes out."

Hannah examined his wounds. "You're lucky, Joey. She could have killed you." She saw his surprise. "I mean it, Joey. If she had kept her wits about her, she could have dropped you where you stood, you and Butch both."

"That's crazy."

Hannah put the small package she had bought into her leather bag, then took out a tube of ointment, which she smeared on Joey's cuts. It stung momentarily, then the pain was gone. The car was filled for a brief time with the smell of wood smoke and mint.

"You don't believe me, do you?" Hannah asked.

Joey shook his head.

"You're lucky," Hannah said again. "You're lucky you're here with me now, with just a few scratches on your face. You could be lying facedown in that herb garden, the life blasted out of you by that old woman's hate."

11

Before finding a place to camp for the night, they stopped at a store to purchase their supper. They remembered to buy a plastic bottle of detergent. Then, following the ridge that climbed above the village, they scouted back roads until they found a logging road that took them off into the woods. Leaving the car in a grove of pines, they traced a sound of running water to its source: a small pool in the rocks below a cascading brook.

Hannah slapped a mosquito. "Perhaps tomorrow we'll splurge on a motel."

"This is great!" Joey replied, immediately setting to work on their campsite. Above the pool the ridge joined a low mountain where light still washed over the hardwoods. Still higher, a rock face flashed as minerals embedded in the stone caught the rays of the late afternoon sun. Down below they were in a cool grotto as private as a room, with space enough to set up camp beside the bubbling water.

They took turns washing, then Joey did a small laundry

and hung his clothes on an improvised rack beside the fire. Hannah put together their supper of cold roast beef and French bread. After they ate, she put on a pot of water for tea.

She glanced several times at Joey as she waited for the water to boil. Butch was already asleep, his legs twitching as he dreamed. At last Hannah took out the small package she had purchased at the herb shop.

"What did you get?" Joey asked.

"It's a kind of tea." She opened the package and poured a brown-green powder into her cup. "Listen, Joey, I'm not sure how this stuff is going to affect me." She poured water into the cup and watched the powder dissolve, stirring it slowly with a spoon. A musty odor spread over the camp, spiced with something sharp that pinched his nose.

Joey shook off his lethargy and sat up straight. "It's not just tea."

Hannah shook her head. "No, it's not." She looked across at him. There was uncertainty in her expression that he could read clearly despite the fading light, and her fear was as visible to him in the fire's faint shadows as it would have been in broad daylight.

"Why drink it?" he asked softly.

She didn't answer. She stirred the brew again with her spoon. Steam rose up into her face. "Whatever happens," she said, "remember your promise." She brought the cup to her lips and sipped the hot drink, then blew on it and sipped again. He watched in silence as she slowly drank the whole cup.

Butch sneezed and looked up, suddenly awake. Hannah placed the empty cup on the ground. She coughed, and a shiver ran through her body.

"Hannah?"

When she turned toward him, her face was glistening with sweat. Her eyes seemed unable to focus on him. "I feel strange," she whispered. "Really strange."

And then as he watched, she closed her eyes and wrapped her arms about her drawn-up knees and sat this way beside the fire, her silver earrings catching the light of the flames, the rest of her a shadow. Butch whined anxiously, but Hannah didn't move. She had gone somewhere, Joey sensed, somewhere they couldn't follow, and he wondered if she would find her way back.

When night came totally, the hill above them faded and a soft wind stirred in the trees around the camp. The fire danced in the moving air and then flared up more brightly. Joey fetched wood and kept a silent vigil beside Hannah's motionless form.

Far away there was a rumble that might have been thunder, a low muttering in hills beyond them. It came no closer, although it seemed to Joey as the night progressed that it moved from one quarter into another. Butch crept near and slept against Joey's leg. Joey must have dozed off too, for suddenly he realized Hannah was on her feet.

"Hannah?" He scrambled up and followed her to the edge of the camp. "Hannah, are you all right?"

She turned toward him, but it was as if she couldn't see him. Her eyes were open but were focused on some inner vision. He took her arm, but she shook him off.

"There is a place of such evil," she whispered, "such pure and festering evil . . ."

"Hannah, come back to the fire."

"To go there is to risk the death of the soul."

His spine went cold as she moaned. Again he tried unsuccessfully to take her arm.

"To enter there is to risk never returning." She sobbed. "I wish I could turn back, oh how I wish I could turn back!"

Before he could stop her, she ran from the campsite into the woods. He ran after her, but he was blind the moment he was beyond the reach of the firelight. He bounced off a tree, cutting his forehead on a jagged branch.

"Hannah!" he shouted.

He stopped to listen. Far off he could hear her steps as branches broke beneath her feet. Butch brushed against his legs.

"Find her," Joey told him. He whipped off his belt and fastened it to the dog's collar. "Hannah, Butch. Go after Hannah."

The dog strained against the belt and Joey followed. Butch seemed to understand, but all Joey could do was trust him blindly, for even Hannah's footsteps were gone now.

They staggered through the woods for what felt like hours. They were clearly climbing up the hill, but everything else was hidden from Joey by the thick night under the trees. Even the sky was at times lost to them. That Butch was following some trail was certain enough, but was it Hannah's trail?

The trees thinned as they climbed higher, and gradually the sky came into view around them. There were no stars, but far off to the south the horizon flashed with reflected lightning. At the edge of a clearing, Butch stopped. He barked. Up ahead Joey saw something move.

"Hannah?" Joey called.

"Go while you can!" she shouted. "Do not follow me any further." Suddenly she sank from sight.

Joey and the dog rushed forward and found her lying on the ground. After making sure she was still breathing, Joey propped her up against a boulder and covered her with his shirt. It would be impossible to try to take her back to camp until first light. As he sat shivering beside her, he held her hand and watched for any sign of waking. Silent lightning played at the edge of the dark sky, and the wind sighed as it came out of the valley below them.

"Don't die, Hannah," he whispered to her. "I won't let you die." It did not occur to him that he had only known this woman since yesterday, and if it had, it would not have changed how he felt. He sat beside her in the night and held her hand tightly and whispered her name, as if in this way he might bring her safely back to him. . . .

When he woke up his hand was empty. Morning had not yet come. He called Butch, but the dog was gone also. He stood up and left the clearing, following the rise of the hill toward its invisible summit, blindly guessing that Hannah must have gone this way. He was in the woods again now, but without Butch he could not see where he was going. When the ground dropped suddenly away below him, he had time for just one desperate backward lunge before he slipped and fell forward into a darkness more total than the night.

12

He lay still, trying to gauge how badly he had hurt himself. He seemed to be at the bottom of a narrow ravine, but when he tentatively searched ahead with one hand, he felt the ground drop off again in front of him. There was no light, but by exploring with his hands he gradually formed a picture of his dilemma: the moss-covered ledge that had stopped his fall, the drop beyond the ledge that might be two feet, or ten, or a hundred.

He rolled carefully over onto his back and looked up toward the sky, but there was only a blackness in that direction, too. He took a deep breath to calm his racing heart. One good thing became apparent as the pain receded: he felt only bruises on his chest and legs, no broken bones.

"Hey, Butch!" he shouted. In the silence he called again. A faint echo mocked him.

He settled in as comfortably as he could, looking upward, waiting for first light. There was nothing he could do until he could see.

He dozed off several times, waking up after each brief respite to find his painful perch on the ledge more uncomfortable than before. It seemed to him impossible that he could sleep in such a place, yet the waves of exhaustion still carried him off and brought him fitful dreams. . . .

"Joey?"

He snapped alert and realized he could see. Night still clung to his ledge, but above him the sky was dull gray. He saw someone up there, looking down at him. Hannah!

"Joey?" she called again.

"Yes, I'm all right." The sound of his voice brought Butch to the edge, where he started barking. Joey's spirits soared at the sight of his dog. "I'm okay," he shouted again.

"Are you sure?"

"Yeah." He worked his way onto his feet. The mossy ledge was barely wide enough to stand on safely, while beyond it he saw the shadows of a further drop. He was about fifteen feet below the top edge of the ravine, where Hannah now peered down on him.

"Can you climb out?"

He looked at the cliff side above him. "No, I don't think so."

"What about the other side?"

"It's too dark to tell yet."

"We'll wait," she said. Her voice sounded normal, deep and strong.

"Are you all right?" he called up to her.

It was a moment before she answered. "Yes."

As they waited for the light to grow, Joey shivered in the morning chill. Perhaps Hannah heard him. When he looked up again, his outer shirt, the one he'd covered Hannah with, came floating down to him. He buttoned it on gratefully.

"Thanks."

"Thank you, Joey," she said. "Can you see yet?"

He looked around. The shape of the far wall of the ravine was becoming clear. If anything, it was steeper and more slippery than the wall above him. When he related this to Hannah, she suggested he follow the ravine lengthwise to see where it led to.

"I'd have to climb down the rest of the way to do that, and then . . ." He tried to brush away the growing panic. He had to keep his head clear. He was only fifteen feet away from safety, even if the cliff was nearly perpendicular and covered with slime. Suddenly he remembered.

"There's a coil of rope in my pack," he shouted up to Hannah. She was already gone, but Butch was still there, looking down at him, whining eagerly, dancing along the edge of the cliff.

"You be careful," Joey called, "or you'll fall in too."

Joey realized Hannah had to go all the way down the hill into camp and then back up again with his rope. There was no way to guess how far they had wandered during the night. He tried to resign himself to the long wait, but as the morning sky brightened above him and the clouds showed streaks of red, he was plagued by a dozen bad thoughts.

What if Hannah got lost and couldn't find their camp? What if she herself fell and twisted her ankle? What if . . .

He tried to shake off his fears. Not since he was little had he depended so much on one person for his immediate safety. It was frightening to need someone this much; it demanded a faith from him that was hard to find.

Butch was barking again. Looking up, Joey saw Hannah at the edge of the cliff. She was uncoiling his rope, lowering one end down to him.

"Tie your end to the thick tree," he told her. He reached

81

up and caught the rope. When she had tied it, he pulled down the slack.

"Be careful," Hannah called to him.

"Yeah." He wished now that he had paid more attention to rope climbing in gym class. After a deep breath, he pulled himself up off the ledge and then braced his feet against the side of the cliff. He managed a yard before his foot slipped. He swung in against the cliff, struck his shoulder, and had to slide down onto the ledge again.

"Tie it under your shoulders," Hannah called to him.

"No," he answered when he realized what she was proposing. "You aren't strong enough to pull me up."

"Maybe not, Joey. But I can keep the rope tight as you climb, keep you from slipping back."

He hesitated.

"Joey, try it."

He looped the rope under his arms and tied it securely where the knot wouldn't interfere with his climbing. "Keep one turn around the tree," he told her. "I'll let you know when to pull in the slack."

He started up. Using the rope as an extra hold, he managed to claw his way to a slippery perch a couple of feet above the ledge. When he shouted, Hannah pulled up the slack in the rope, providing him with a second firm grip. He found another stance a little above the first. As soon as the rope was again taut, he climbed on toward a small crack that ran diagonally across the top face of the cliff. When he slipped, his body took up the slack with a heavy jolt. But the rope held him. He scrambled his way back onto the rock.

"Hannah?"

"I'm okay, Joey. Go on!"

This time he reached the crack, and after a brief rest, he

pulled his way up to the lip and wriggled over. He lay facedown on the ground for a moment, catching his breath. Butch burrowed into him and licked his face.

He rolled over and hugged the dog and looked up at Hannah. She was still holding the rope. Her face was gray.

"You did it, Hannah," he said.

Her skirt was torn from her night in the woods, and her hair had come down. It lay in a tangle about her face. But no one had ever looked more beautiful to him before in his whole life.

"Well, did you think I was going to leave you stranded down there?" she asked gruffly.

He laughed and stood up. "I'm glad to see you again." He studied her to see if she had been changed any by the tea that had drugged her, but except for her pallor, she looked the same as before.

Her eyes met his and did not waver. He looked down finally at Butch, who was tugging on the cuffs of Joey's muddy jeans. Joey bent down to remove the belt still looped around Butch's collar.

Hannah had coiled up the rope, and now she handed it to him. "Let's get some sleep," she said. "We're going to need it."

Joey slept until mid-morning. He awoke when the sun broke through the clouds, stabbing into their camp like a beacon. He sat up to find that Hannah had packed away all the gear, including the clothes he had washed the evening before. She was sitting by the smoldering fire, studying the picture of his mother that he carried in his pack. When she realized he was awake, she looked over at him.

"Who's this?" she asked.

"My mother."

"You look like her." Hannah did not appear concerned that he had caught her with the photograph. She leaned over and slipped it back into his pack.

"She's dead," Joey said.

Hannah nodded. She threw him a dry pair of jeans and busied herself dousing the fire while he dressed. In a few minutes they were back on the dirt road, driving off the ridge into the valley.

"Where are we going today?" Joey asked, getting out the map.

Hannah kept her eyes on the road ahead. "Abaddon Woods. It's in the White Mountains." She reached over and stabbed the map with one finger, near the green area that represented the National Forest. "It's not on the map, but we'll find it."

"And what's there?"

Hannah didn't answer. They stopped for breakfast soon after that, and while they ate, she remained silent. Back in the car she hummed as she drove, a low, plaintive melody Joey had never heard before.

13

On the way north through the mountains, Joey napped and woke to find the heat a smoky haze around them. High thunderheads were wedged into the sky. Between their towering bulks, the sun poured down its fire, fueling the currents that fed the clouds above the rolling hills.

He glanced at Hannah. If she was exhausted from the night she had spent in the trance, wandering the hillside, she wasn't giving in to it. Except for the paleness of her face and a tightening of the lines around her mouth, she seemed unchanged. She hardly rested, hardly took in any nourishment. To Joey it was clear that she was racing against time. But what was she searching for? And what did she hope to find in Abaddon Woods?

Joey ached from his fall into the ravine. While dressing that morning, he had seen the ugly bruises on his legs and body.

He stretched now to relieve the kinks in his muscles. "Are we close?"

Hannah nodded but said nothing. Joey listened to the noises in the engine each time the car labored up a hill. They were getting louder. Sometimes, near the top of a rise when Hannah was forced to shift down into first, Joey thought the engine was going to pound apart. It was so bad he didn't dare point it out to Hannah. She could surely hear it herself. When they stopped for gas, the attendant added two quarts of oil.

As they drove on, Joey tried to figure out what day it was. Time had taken on a strange, uneven quality—sometimes drifting by, sometimes speeding. He watched the heavy traffic pass them, and counting back, discovered it was Friday. He had left Boston on Tuesday. It seemed more like a month ago.

In the early afternoon, Hannah turned off the pavement and followed a dirt road that wound its way into the hills. There were no signboards, yet the way seemed clear to her. At each fork in the road she would hesitate for just a moment before making her choice, left or right; she took no longer deciding whether or not to turn onto a side road.

"Feels like we're going in circles," Joey said, tasting the dust that poured in through the windows.

Hannah grunted. The engine rapped loudly now on each hill; the car trembled on the washboard roads. She drove on with no show of concern. Only her white knuckles where she gripped the steering wheel betrayed her tension.

They stopped at a wide place where the road ended. Hannah backed the car around and faced it out. She switched off the engine and looked around.

"The way to Abaddon Woods is up that logging road," she said. She looked at Joey. "Why don't you wait for me here?"

Joey shook his head. "Why should I?"

Hannah shrugged. "You may be sorry if you come."

Puzzled, but determined not to be persuaded to stay behind, Joey climbed out of the car and began to shoulder his pack.

"Leave that," Hannah told him. "We'll not be staying long in Abaddon Woods."

The logging road led through a spruce forest. As the road climbed, hardwoods gradually took over, until, when they crossed the shoulder of a ridge, they found themselves deep in a section of tall beech trees and oaks. Sunlight slipped through the leaves and dappled the ground around them, forming dancing, windy patterns in their eyes. Above the deep hush of the forest, Joey heard the wind brushing the treetops with a sound like far-off waves. As they followed the dimly outlined road deeper into the woods, Butch trotted ahead of them, sniffing out a multitude of details too subtle for their own senses.

Several miles in, the road petered out and became an indistinct trail. Hannah hardly broke stride as she followed it into the deeper gloom of a marsh. The trees now were stained with lichen, and the damp odor of rot saturated the air.

At times Joey lost sight of the trail altogether, but Hannah each time found it again: beyond a wet place or around the far side of a rocky knoll. Above the trees the sky grew dark with clouds, and Joey heard the rumble of distant thunder. But no wind stirred the forest floor. The heavy air pressed in upon them as if to stop them from going any farther.

Joey was sweating heavily; yet he felt cold. Up ahead, Butch had stopped on the crest of a slight hill. When they caught up, Joey realized the trees were thinning. Beyond lay a field and the remains of an apple orchard. At its far edge a house brooded in the gray glare below the thunderheads. There was a barn to one side, and in the field several goats were tethered to stakes.

Butch growled. Joey looked down and was surprised to see the hair standing up on the dog's back. "Easy, Butch," he told him. "They're just goats."

But it wasn't the grazing animals that troubled Butch. By the time they reached the edge of the orchard nearest the house, he was flattened belly-down against the ground and would go no further.

"Come on, Butch," Joey called to him.

The dog yawned several times, but wouldn't follow. Saliva dripped from his mouth.

"He's really scared," Joey told Hannah.

She glanced at the dog, then back at the house. A powerfully built man dressed in a white, billowing shirt had come out on the front porch, above a flight of stone steps. He stood there regarding them. His head was totally without hair.

"Wait here," Hannah said. She left Joey by the orchard. As she climbed the stone steps to the porch, the bald man turned on his heels and went back into the house. Joey watched Hannah follow him inside.

He went back to Butch. The dog stuck a wet snout into his hands. "It's okay, boy," Joey soothed him. "You're right. It's strange here."

From his crouch he looked around at the decaying apple trees, at the distant goats in the field. It should have been a normal country scene, and yet it wasn't. Something was wrong with it, something he could sense but not quite discover. When Butch began to growl again, Joey turned and saw a pair of skinny legs. He straightened up quickly. A girl was standing a few feet from them.

"Sorry, I didn't hear you come up," Joey told her.

She was close to his age, maybe a year older, very thin, with dark red hair that flowed long down her back. Her skin was a pale white beside the scarlet of her lips, and Joey wondered if she was wearing lipstick. She made no move to introduce herself.

Joey extended his hand. "I'm Joey Carr," he told her.

She ignored the offer to shake hands. "I know that. Hannah told me who you are." Her voice was a thin whine. It set his teeth on edge. "And is this the famous Butch?" she asked scornfully. "He doesn't look like much."

Joey looked at his dog, then back at the girl. With a dozen retorts on the tip of his tongue, he chose to say nothing.

"I'm to entertain you," the girl said airily. "While Hannah does business with my father."

"Was that your father on the porch?"

The girl laughed. It was a musical sound compared to the whine of her voice. Joey had the distinct feeling that the voice she was using was an imitation, not her real voice at all.

"Oh no, Joey. That was Hans. My father never comes outside. He's an eccentric." She laughed again. "He's so rich and powerful he doesn't have to leave the house for anything. Everything comes to him."

Butch growled. Joey bent over to quiet him.

"How shall I entertain you?" the girl asked. "Do you play games?"

Joey shrugged.

"How about hide-and-seek?"

"That's for kids."

"Not always." She made a face. "Very well. At least come and look at the dogs."

She led the way around the barn to a kennel in the back.

Behind a wire fence two huge German shepherds paced their dirt compound. Butch stayed behind Joey's legs, barking furiously at the two dogs inside the fence. The girl looked at him with an impatient shake of her head.

"Do shut him up, Joey. Those are our hunting dogs. They don't bark at all."

Joey watched the dogs paw at the ground behind their fence, as if to dig their way out. They had not uttered a sound.

"I'll hide in the barn," the girl said suddenly. "You find me."

Before he could protest, she ran off. Reluctantly, he waited there by the kennel to give her time to hide. The German shepherds had stopped their futile digging and were staring at him steadily through the wire. Even Butch had stopped barking, as if their strange refusal to bark back had silenced him.

The girl's laughter came floating to him from the direction of the barn. Slowly he turned away from the kennel and went to look for her.

He searched the ground floor of the barn but did not find her. Stairs took him up to a second floor crowded with the cast-off furniture of several generations. Joey walked down narrow rows between old chairs and ancient bedsteads. Everything was covered with a thick dust that swirled up in his passing and stretched in clouds across the beams of light that filtered through the broken shutters on the windows.

He followed footsteps on the dirty floor to a narrow door in back. Opening it, he discovered a small room that had once been used as living quarters. A rolltop desk leaned against one wall. A bed in the middle of the room was covered with a tent of sheets. He heard a movement and turned toward the darkest corner of the room. He saw the girl hanging from a large hook in the ceiling. A frayed rope was wound tightly around her neck and her face was blue and swollen.

For a moment he was too startled to move. Then he rushed forward to pull her down. As his hands touched her, she suddenly swung free and dropped to the floor, peals of her laughter filling the shabby room.

"I was holding myself there the whole time. I thought you'd never find me."

"Very funny." He turned and walked out into the storage area. She followed him, still laughing. He stared at her neck, which was red with rope burns.

"I had to make it look real," she told him. "That was the fun of it."

Downstairs, Butch jumped all over him. Joey started for the doorway.

"Wait, Joey. It's your turn to hide now."

"No."

"You're no fun."

He whirled on her to say something angry, for he was still shaking. Before he could get a word out, she leaned forward and kissed him.

"There, does that make it better?"

Speechless, he stood looking at her. Behind him someone entered the barn.

"Come on, Joey," Hannah said. "We're leaving now."

"Don't go," the girl begged. Her laughter now was gone. Her eyes were wide with sadness. "Stay."

He followed Hannah and Butch out into the yard. When he looked back from the orchard, the girl was still standing in the doorway of the barn, her face white against the shadows behind her. Then Hannah urged him on, and he hurried to catch up.

14

Thunder rumbled overhead as they recrossed the marsh. Glimpses of the sky above the trees revealed black storm clouds, and the light within the woods was quickly fading. Hannah set a fast pace along the path, impatiently searching the ground ahead whenever she lost the way.

"How did you make out with that girl's father?" Joey asked when they were a good mile away from the house.

Hannah looked sideways at him, then at the path ahead. "The price he wanted was too high, Joey. Far too high."

"For what?" Joey asked in frustration. "I just don't understand what you're looking for."

"Isn't it clear by now?" she asked angrily. "Isn't it plain enough, for God's sake?"

When he said nothing, she shook her head. "I've no time to explain it now. We have to get back to the car."

"It's only a thunderstorm."

"It's not the storm I'm worried about." She didn't take time to elaborate. "Hurry, Joey!"

Either because of the poor light, or because they were traveling so fast, it soon became clear they had lost the way.

"We'll spread out," Hannah told him. She waved him to the left. "Crisscross back and forth. We've got to find that path."

They continued walking in what they hoped was the correct direction, searching left and right for the path. Beyond the swamp, Joey saw an opening in the trees and hurried toward it. The wind gusted heavily through the branches above him, while behind him in the swamp, two trees rubbed their trunks together, giving out a tortured sound.

"Hannah!" he shouted. "It's the logging road."

She crossed to where he waited and hugged him. "Good boy, Joey."

As they raced along the road, Butch lingered behind. Several times Joey had to stop to wait for him. The dog kept turning to face the way they had come, and the hair again was up on his back.

"Come on, Butch," Joey called to him. "We're going to get drenched."

The light in the woods now was purple with reflections from the thick clouds overhead. Lightning slashed the sky, with thunder booming close behind. The wind drowned out their voices when they tried to talk.

"Hurry up, Joey," Hannah shouted. "The car isn't much farther."

He was barely keeping up with her. Her long skirt swirled around her legs as she ran along the logging road. When he stopped once more to wait for Butch, she shouted at him to leave the dog.

"I can't," he shouted back. The wind broke a tree branch above him. He ducked instinctively. Before the branch could fall on him, it wedged itself in the fork of another tree.

Then in the flash of a lightning bolt he saw them: the two German shepherds from the kennel.

Noses to the ground, they were following the logging road. They were still a quarter of a mile back when he first saw them, running silently, without barking.

"Butch!" he shouted.

His dog turned and came to him. Together they hurried to catch up with Hannah, but again Butch stopped to look back. Beyond Hannah, Joey saw the car at the edge of the woods.

"Let's go, Butch. We're almost there."

Looking over his shoulder, Joey saw that one of the German shepherds was rapidly closing the distance between them, loping ahead in quick, deadly strides that ate up their margin of safety. The car was too far away. . . .

Before the German shepherd could reach them, Butch circled around and charged.

"Butch, no!" Joey started back to pull Butch free, but then Hannah was holding his arm, preventing him from going to the dog's rescue.

"Leave him, Joey!" she cried. "It's the only way."

She was dragging him toward the car with a strength born of her desperation. He could not shake her off. He saw the other German shepherd join the fight, and he knew then that it was hopeless. They tumbled over Butch like wolves. His dog fought bravely, but he was outnumbered and overmatched. He was lost in the swirl of their legs, the fury of their teeth.

And still Joey would have charged into the fight in futile rage had not Hannah pulled him toward the car.

"You can't save him," she said. "You can't."

She would not release him. Her strength was a match for his. Too brokenhearted finally to resist any longer, he allowed himself to go with her.

They reached the car as the rain dropped out of the sky. Hannah started the engine and switched on the headlights. As they rolled ahead, the two German shepherds broke onto the road. Hannah gunned the engine and drove by them, but not before Joey saw that one of them had a red slash on his chest. Butch had struck home at least once in his own defense. Then the dogs were gone, and he and Hannah were alone on the rain swept road.

As they wound their way through the labyrinth toward the main road, Joey sat in silence, his head whirling with thoughts too swift and painful to put into words.

"He did it to save you," Hannah said at last. "To have refused his sacrifice would have been the cruelest thing you could have done."

"I should have tried to help him," Joey whispered.

Hannah reached over to touch his knee. "No, Joey. You couldn't have saved him, and then the dogs would have attacked you. Butch bought us time to reach the car, bought it with his own life, freely given. Some gifts you have to accept, Joey. To refuse them is a sacrilege."

The wipers slapped across the windshield. The rain descended from the sky in torrents, as if to wash the ground clean of Butch's blood.

15

They stopped for supper in a small tourist town north of the White Mountain National Forest. The narrow street of neon lights, smeared by the rain, was reflected brightly in a thousand puddles. In the diner Hannah for once ate heartily, as if their escape from Abaddon Woods had stirred her appetite. Joey munched drily on a hamburger, played with his French fries.

Hannah reached over and squeezed his hand. "Eat, Joey."

He shook his head and pushed away his plate. "Where are we going to camp tonight?"

"We're not." Hannah burped several times and finished her coffee. "We're treating ourselves to a motel tonight, and showers, and dry beds."

Joey looked at the greasy counter. "I haven't enough money left for a motel."

"Then you'll be my guest."

He shook his head. "You go to a motel. I'll find a place to

camp, and you can pick me up in the morning. It's almost stopped raining."

"Do you know that you can be quite difficult at times?" Hannah ordered another cup of coffee. "Dear, but difficult. We're going to a motel on my money and that's all there is to it. I'll not have you moping around in a wet sleeping bag all night and catching cold and . . ."

"I'm not moping."

"Really? I think you're feeling sorry for yourself. Instead of being proud of your dog for what he did, you're wasting your time on self-pity."

He glared at her. "What do you know about it?"

"About self-pity? A little while ago I could have written a book about it."

He looked at her in the silence that fell between them. He could hear the buzz of voices around them in the restaurant. Outside, cars drove by in an endless chain of lights.

"Really, Joey, wouldn't you rather take a shower and climb into a clean bed tonight, instead of stumbling around in the dark trying to set up camp, waking up tomorrow to discover you're in someone's backyard?"

He had to smile at her picture of it. "Yeah."

"Good. Then it's settled."

Outside, they found that the rain had stopped. Drops fell from trees, striking single notes as they hit the ground. Joey looked around to call Butch, then remembered.

They found a motel to fit their finances on a side road a few miles from the diner. It was a small cabin colony that had survived from an earlier day. A halfhearted effort had been made to bring it up-to-date with battered air conditioners and secondhand television sets.

When they had carried inside the things they needed from

the car, they took turns with the shower. Joey closed his eyes and felt the cool sting of the water stripping the grime and fatigue from his body.

Afterward, they sat out in front of their cabin on two wooden lawn chairs and watched the remnants of the storms drift away toward the horizon. They talked quietly. Then Hannah cleared her throat and leaned forward.

"I guess I owe you a bit of an explanation, after what happened today," she said.

Joey shrugged. "You don't owe me anything."

"I won't burden you with much of it," she went on, "but you did ask me today what I'm looking for. I find it hard to believe you haven't formed an idea of it by now."

Joey looked along the glistening lawn toward the road, where a truck shifted gears as it drove by. "Maybe," he said.

"Are you afraid we'll offend someone if we mention it out loud?"

"You're the one who's been vague," Joey answered. "I've asked you at least a couple of times."

She grunted. "That's true." She sighed and settled back in her chair. "I'm looking for an answer, Joey. An answer to a riddle that my body decided to pose to me about a year ago. And the riddle is, why does an otherwise healthy woman in the prime of her life suddenly decide to get sick and die? Do you have any clues on that one, Joey?"

"No." He glanced over at her and saw the strange smile on her face. "I'm not big on answers. I came up with the idea of running away to my grandparents' place, leaving my dad alone like he wants to be, but that's about the best I've been able to do lately."

Hannah laughed softly. "Do you have doubts about it now?"

"Maybe."

"Because of what happened today? That was my fault."

Joey shook his head. "You told me to wait at the car. I wanted to go with you."

"So you accept full responsibility for the choice you made?"

"Yes."

"But you didn't know what you were faced with, so how could you be responsible?"

"I don't know." Joey felt tears in his eyes and looked out over the lawn again. "I don't know."

"Joey, I'm just talking around things instead of going to the heart of the matter. The point is, I'm looking for an answer to my cancer, something other than the death that the doctors promise me. Call it a cure, or another choice, call it whatever you like."

"In Abaddon Woods?" Joey asked. "In drugged tea?"

Hannah stared at him. "Well, where I choose to look is my business," she said softly. "But I've no right to expose you to danger."

"No sweat."

"Don't be flip with me!"

He realized she was crying. "I'm sorry," he said quickly.

She ignored his apology. "Don't hide behind smart-ass remarks, Joey. The things that are happening here are real. They can hurt us, they can change us. If you waste your time on pretense, you'll misunderstand everything, including the real dangers. And there *are* real dangers here."

"I'm sorry," he repeated. "I didn't mean to sound that way."

It was several moments before she spoke again. "I have just one more stop to make between here and your grandparents' house in Vermont, and that stop is directly on our way. If you want to split up here and go on alone, I'll understand, especially after what happened today. But if you want to go on with me, I promise to take you directly to your grandparents' house the day after tomorrow."

Joey nodded. "Okay."

"You're sure?"

"Yes."

She took his hand and squeezed it. "I'm glad I met you Joey."

"I'm glad I met you," he said. And despite what had happened to Butch, he knew it was true.

After Hannah went into the cabin, he stayed outside awhile longer. He thought over all the things that had happened in the past few days and tried to sort them out and make sense of them. Butch was gone, and now the words of the Gypsy girl's prophecy glowed in his mind as if spelled out by burning sticks. He whispered them softly to himself:

> *"Soon in your life*
> *with two you'll deal.*
> *One will die,*
> *the other reveal."*

Clearly Butch was the one who died. And Hannah was the other. But what had she revealed to him except things that confused him? That she thought she was a witch he had no doubt. But that she really had any gifts in magic, he doubted very much. Abaddon Woods was an evil place, but no more so than many other places in the world at various times.

And yet . . .

There was something going on that he couldn't point to and say, there, that's it, that's the truth of what's happening here. He couldn't assign a shape to recent events, yet he sensed something important nonetheless. Magic, witch-craft, good and evil—these words did not explain it. What was happening was under the words; raw and crude and quite real, even if the language to describe it eluded him.

But understanding it was vital. He sensed that his whole life might depend on coming to grips with these vague shadows.

The night was still now, all mutterings of the storms gone over the horizon. He watched a rabbit steal onto the lawn and begin nibbling at the wet grass. He could hear the sound of its teeth as it calmly ate its fill. The hour was late and he was tired, yet he remained sitting there, spellbound by the peacefulness of the rabbit's night meal.

He considered what Hannah had just told him, about her quest for a cure. Her daring and her courage in the face of such bleak odds confused him. She was clearly not a fool, yet what hope had she of finding anything at all to save her here in the backwaters of New England?

He stood up. At the door he looked in before entering. Hannah was sitting cross-legged on her bed in a long flannel nightgown. She had cut a piece of rope from the coil he carried in his pack. Her mouth was moving silently as she carefully tied knots in the rope, one knot after another, along its whole length.

He watched for a while, then tiptoed away to go for a walk.

16

Joey woke up several times during the night to hear Hannah tossing on the other bed, moaning softly. Every time she climbed out of bed to go to the bathroom, she left the light off in order not to wake him, but he was awake each time. He heard her rummaging through her leather bag, heard her draw a glass of water. When finally her breathing became regular and even, first light was creeping in at the windows.

They got off to a late start in the morning and did not cross into Vermont until shortly after noon. It was Saturday, but they had left the tourists behind and traffic was light.

"It's getting worse," Hannah said as they drove along an empty tarred road between acres of scrubby pines and fir trees. The scars from a recent fire were still apparent on the land. Many of the trees were charred, their needles scorched brown, their lower branches bare.

"What's getting worse?" Joey asked.

"The engine. That terrible noise."

Joey listened. The rapping was louder than yesterday. Whatever was wrong, it was clearly getting worse. At the next town they added more oil, but it did nothing to muffle the destructive sounds within the engine.

The chill from the night's rain burned off quickly, and the afternoon was as hot as yesterday, maybe hotter. Joey was tired of riding, tired of their crawling progress up and down hills, any of which threatened to be the last one the ancient car would survive.

He tried to interest himself in the farms and fields they passed, in the patches of corn that quilted the hills, but he felt strangely uneasy. He missed Butch, missed his persistent wet nose and his excitement at each stop they made along their journey. It seemed wrong to be going on without him, and despite the fact that the map clearly proved they were getting closer and closer to his grandparents' home in Carverville, he felt as if they were getting no closer at all.

Hannah glanced across at him several times. Even with the hour she had spent this morning over her hair and her makeup, her choice of earrings and bracelets, she was beginning to show the strain of the past few days. Her face was pale; the lines there more deeply creased her skin. Her bracelets rattled over wrists that were nothing more than bone.

"Do you sense it?" she asked.

"What?"

But she didn't answer. She swerved to avoid a large, red fox that darted suddenly out of a gully beside the road and crossed in front of them. At the edge of the woods it turned to watch them pass.

Hannah mumbled to herself and gripped the wheel more tightly.

They drove into Hollington, Vermont as the thunderheads began massing again above the surrounding hills. The streets of the small city were narrow, lined with dilapidated two-and three-decker wooden apartment buildings. Porches sagged ominously above alleyways clogged with old cars and piles of refuse.

Beside the river that cut the town in two, a paper mill sent columns of rank steam high against the hills. The air was thick with the taste of something acid, something subtly corrosive; and the heat seemed doubled by the absence of any lawns or shrubs or trees.

Hannah consulted an address on a piece of paper as they drove slowly through street after street. The houses all looked identical to Joey, as if a film lay over everything, robbing each building of any color or distinction it might have once had.

The house they stopped at was no different from the others, except for a small sign in one front window:

BOOKS
Bought and Sold
MR. A. GROSS, PROP.

Hannah shut off the engine. The silence that followed was such a relief, they both sat without moving for several minutes. Finally, Hannah reached for her leather bag and got out.

"Don't stray off too far," she said. "I won't be long."

Joey watched her walk up to the front door. She rang the bell several times before at last the door opened and she slipped inside, without revealing a glimpse to Joey of the person who had opened it for her.

The street baked in the afternoon heat. From the direction of the mill came a muffled rumble of machinery. Joey got out of the car and walked toward the river. Several times he turned to look back, so strong was his feeling of being followed. But each time the street behind him was empty.

He paused on the bridge over the river to watch the clots of dirty brown foam drift by under him. The smell was stronger. The rumble from the mill crowded the narrow street, overfilling it. He heard his name whispered and whirled around, but no one was there. At the far corner of the street an old woman appeared, pulling a shopping cart.

It had been a quirk, he decided. A vibration set up in his ears by the noise from the mill. He walked on toward the center of town, still sensing that he was being followed but refusing to turn around again.

Two blocks from the main street of Hollington he saw Butch sitting in front of an abandoned movie theater. Joey rubbed the sweat out of his eyes and looked again. It was either Butch or his twin: same color, same size, same peculiar mismatch of head and legs. Joey started running.

"Butch!" he shouted. "Hey, Butch, it's me!"

The dog stood up and wagged its tail. Then, before Joey could reach it, the dog turned and trotted into the alleyway between the theater and the dry cleaner's shop next to it.

"Wait, Butch," Joey shouted. There was a nagging thought at the back of his mind, the realization that this dog hadn't barked and Butch would surely have barked upon seeing him again. But Joey pushed away his doubts, for he wanted to believe, wanted this dog to be his dog. He turned the corner and ran up the alley.

There was no sign of the dog. The alley ended in a blank brick wall. Just this side of the wall, a door into the theater stood open, leaning crookedly on its hinges. Without stopping to consider, Joey plunged inside.

He followed a corridor to an open archway into the theater itself, where the rows and rows of seats were faintly visible in the dim light that drifted down from the high, vaulted ceiling. Two balconies curved above him, sagging perilously in their centers; and at the other end, in front of the screen that had peeled away in strips, wood scaffolding crisscrossed its way up to a huge crystal chandelier.

The musty smell of rot filled his nose. He threaded his way between the seats, through a rubble of torn upholstery, to the central aisle.

"Butch?" he called. His voice echoed from the cavernous ceiling. He looked up. A breeze from somewhere above was rippling through the chandelier, setting the hundreds of glass beads in motion like a giant wind chime. Their liquid notes filled the theater. Below, under the scaffolding, something moved.

"Butch, it's me." As Joey hurried forward, his right shoulder struck one of the uprights holding the scaffolding in place. He felt it give way, heard the tortured rending of boards coming loose above him.

He hesitated for a moment. The universe was falling apart around him. He dove under a workbench as the scaffolding collapsed, sending down a cascade of heavy timbers, thick boards, and finally the chandelier itself, which broke in a barrage of crystal splinters in the chaos all around him.

It was a long time before he trusted that he was still alive. The workbench had saved him, dividing the falling timbers as a rock divides the waters of a stream. he was choking on the dust that had been raised up, his heart was threatening to pound itself out through his chest, but he had hardly a scratch on him as witness to his close call.

During the time that it took him to crawl through the wreckage, he forgot about seeing Butch. But once clear, he remembered, and he searched every foot of the theater before he gave up.

Disappointed, he headed toward the corridor that he had followed in from the alley. It seemed hard to believe that another dog could look so much like Butch, but Butch would not have run from him. Yet where had he gone, this dog who looked enough like Butch to be his twin?

In the corridor Joey saw a figure looking in at him from the doorway, silhouetted against the glare of the brick wall outside.

"I'm all right," he called. "The . . ."

Before he could finish, the figure whirled around and ran, but he had time enough to see long hair and pipe-thin legs. The girl from Abaddon Woods!

He ran outside, but the alley was empty. In the street beyond, only strangers walked by. He looked both ways, blinking in the bright light, but the girl was gone. If she had ever been there. . . .

He shook his head as he dusted off his clothes. Someone had been in the doorway as he came out, that was certain. But how could he be sure that the figure he had seen in the glare of light from the alley was the girl from Abaddon Woods? He had not really seen her face; he had just had time enough to notice her long hair and thin legs. And what would she be doing here in Vermont?

But certain things stuck fast in his mind as he hurried back toward the car. Strongest among them was the clear memory of a dog who looked exactly like Butch, but who turned away from him without barking, as silent as the killer dogs in Abaddon Woods.

17

Hannah was sitting in the car, reading a large book propped up against the steering wheel. She glanced at him as he got in beside her, sighed and closed the book. Joey caught a glimpse of its title before she stuffed it into her leather bag and pulled tight the drawstring.

"What language is that?" he asked.

"French."

"Is it what you're looking for?"

"No, but it will help us tonight." She didn't explain. "Are you all right?"

Quickly he told her what had happened inside the old movie theater. As he talked, she watched some papers blow by the car, on a gust of wind that came from the river.

"You were a fool to go in there," she told him.

"The dog looked so much like Butch and . . ."

"Do you really think he survived those German shepherds?" She stared at him. "Do you?"

"It's possible."

She shook her head. "He didn't. Listen, Joey, some things can be changed and some are finished. Your dog is gone. He died at the edge of Abaddon Woods yesterday, and no amount of wishful thinking is going to bring him back."

"All right," Joey said angrily.

Her face softened. "It's just that until you can accept it, you won't be able to let go of him."

"Well, I'm sure of the girl," Joey said to change the subject. "It was the girl from Abaddon Woods who was looking in at me from the alley doorway."

Hannah nodded. She started the car and drove slowly through the light traffic out of the city. As Hollington dropped away behind them, the wind followed, up from the river valley below, throwing itself against the tree-covered hills. On exposed curves, the car rocked in the gusts, and Hannah had to wrestle the wheel to keep from going off the road.

"Going to storm again," Joey said, gazing through his window at the copper-colored sky. The tops of the thunderheads were lost in the haze above, but their bases loomed large and close, swollen with rain.

They stopped to eat supper at a small roadside restaurant. They were high in the hills now, heading north toward his grandparents' home by the lake in Carverville, deep in the Northeast Kingdom of Vermont. Joey rolled the words over and over in his mind. They had a magic in them, a special flavor. And a few miles beyond the lake where his grandparents lived was the Canadian border. This also held a magic for him: a sense of an edge to things, an edge to life itself. The border was a line that could be crossed, leaving the past behind, welcoming the future. . . .

A loud crash brought him out of his dreams. A tree limb

had come down in the wind and smashed into one of the restaurant's windows. The overweight cook hurried across the dining room to see how much damage had been done.

"Let's go," Hannah told Joey. She paid the cashier, who couldn't take her eyes off the broken window.

"Gonna be a wild night," she said. She punched buttons on the cash register without looking. "We get some real bad storms up here."

Outside, the clouds had turned an ugly purple, like bruises in the sky. The neon sign in front of the restaurant shook in the wind.

"Are we going to a motel?" Joey shouted.

Hannah shook her head. "Not tonight."

They got into the car. "Are we broke?" Joey asked.

"Not quite," Hannah said. "We could afford another night at a motel, but we need something more private tonight."

The question died on Joey's lips as they left the restaurant behind. By now he had learned that Hannah explained whatever she wanted to explain, and nothing more.

Searching the dirt roads, they found a deserted lean-to, open on one side, by itself near a cellar hole. In the last murky light of evening they set up camp inside, hanging Joey's storm tarp in case the roof leaked, which Joey thought probable since he could see the sky through it. Rain seemed imminent; thunder already rumbled in the hills, and the trees above the shed bent in gusts of wind.

Hannah built a large fire in the shelter of some rocks near the cellar hole. She walked back and forth between the fire and the shed, brewing tea. Her long skirt swirled in the wind, and when her hair blew loose, she took out a scarf and tied her hair back. In the dancing firelight she looked like a Gypsy.

110

"Here, drink this," she said, bringing him a cup.

Remembering the tea she had drunk the night after visiting Aunt Maddy's herb shop, he regarded the cup suspiciously.

Hannah laughed. "It won't hurt you, Joey." She returned to the fire and brought back a cup for herself, then broke out a tin of crackers from her stores in the car. They sat munching the crackers and sipping their tea as night settled around their camp. Joey was reassured by the taste of the tea and had a second cup.

He grew sleepy as Hannah tended the fire. He wondered why she had built it so far from the shed.

"Joey?"

He shook his head to clear it and looked up at her. She crouched down until her face was inches from his. Her earrings caught the light of the fire and flashed as they swung from side to side.

"Listen to me, Joey. You'll be asleep soon, but first you must understand something."

He tried to speak, struggling with a tongue that now felt too heavy and thick to move. "You drugged my tea," he managed to say. "You lied to me."

She shook her head. The earrings flashed, her face began to spin. "I didn't lie. I said the tea wouldn't hurt you and it won't. On the contrary, the potion I put in your cup will protect you."

"Potion? I . . ."

"Be quiet, Joey. There isn't much time."

She was so close he could feel her breath on his face. He fought to keep his eyes open.

"We have been followed by evil ever since we left Abaddon Woods." She squeezed his knee to keep him awake. "It's time we freed ourselves from it. We can't go on until we

111

do. Listen, Joey. If the potion fails, if for any reason you wake up before you should, do not speak to me. Understand, Joey? No matter what you see, do not say a word, do not interrupt, do not move from this shed."

He tried to nod but his head was a lump of rock. His neck ached with the weight of it. He wanted to lie down, close his eyes, give in to his incredible need for sleep.

But he forced himself to stay awake as Hannah took a cloth bundle from her leather bag and unwrapped a curious knife with a long, curved blade. Numbly he watched her step outside. On a level stretch of bare earth between the fire and the shed, she drew a large circle with the knife.

She turned to look his way. "Go to sleep," she commanded.

He saw her body weave in the firelight as she drew figures in the circle. Then the waves of sleep were too strong for him, and he sank into soft darkness that went on and on and down and down. . . .

He dreamed that somewhere in the darkness a bridge appeared, illuminated by the moon and stretching toward a narrow point of light too far away to guess its distance. As Joey approached, he saw Butch on the near side of the bridge, one of his paws caught in the ugly teeth of a steel trap. Joey ran to free him, but he slipped on the ramp leading to the bridge and fell back.

Again and again Joey tried to leap up the ramp to the bridge where Butch waited for him. Each time he slipped and fell. Then he saw the girl from Abaddon Woods. She was climbing down the suspension wires of the bridge, like a spider down its web. Joey knew that if she reached Butch first, all would be lost.

He threw himself upon the ramp again, his fingers clawing at its glasslike surface. He heard his name and saw Hannah on the bridge above him.

"Help Butch," he shouted to her, but she shook her head.

"You must do it yourself," she said. "And you can, Joey. You must."

The girl was nearly down from the wires. Her lips were drawn back in a scarlet smile. Joey groaned and circled around the ramp to the stone abutment of the bridge itself. He found a handhold and started climbing.

Below him in a chasm, a river roared over unseen rocks. At the top of the abutment, he could find no final hold. He had to leap blindly. His fingers caught on the top edge, and in a moment more he had pulled himself over. Just ahead of the girl, he reached Butch and freed him from the trap.

Butch licked his face and then was away, racing ahead of the girl over the bridge toward the brilliant light at the far side. She could only follow him part of the way and then she stopped, while Butch raced on, ever smaller and smaller, until he disappeared into the light and was gone. . . .

Joey woke up soaked with sweat, tangled in a blanket that Hannah must have thrown over him. The first thing he was aware of was the silence, and as he sat up with a throbbing head, he realized that the wind had stopped. Beyond the open side of the shed, he saw stars spread across the night sky. The storms were gone, and the air felt cool and clean on his face.

Hannah was lightly snoring in the other corner of the shed, a bundle of blankets wrapped around her. Joey stood up and made his way unsteadily outside. The fire smoldered in its ashes. He bent over it and threw in some fresh sticks of wood, stirring it to life. He remembered then what had happened before he slept and realized he had just walked through the circle Hannah had drawn on the ground. But when he looked back, he could see no sign of the circle on the bare dirt between the fire and the shed.

Puzzled, his mind still cloudy with sleep and fragments of the dream, he studied the ground. The entire area had been brushed smooth. Joey found the branch Hannah had used as a rake on the far side of the clearing. Only his own fresh footprints marred the dirt. Whatever had happened here tonight, she had taken care to erase all signs of it.

Joey looked up at the sky, now empty of clouds, a field of stars. Only the faintest breeze stirred in the trees. He remembered his dream, remembered the way Butch, once he was free, had raced across the bridge to safety, to the light on the other side.

Joey shook his head. Maybe he would never understand all that had happened to him since meeting Hannah, but he knew it was good. In the depths of his heart, he knew it was good.

Part Three

THE ROAD
ENDS

18

They ate a light breakfast of crackers and tea while birds called from the trees. An early chill hovered close to the ground, while overhead the sky was a solid, unbroken arch of blue. Still sleepy from the drug Hannah had put in his tea last night, Joey tried to rub the blur from his eyes as he squatted near the low-burning fire.

"It's Sunday, Joey," Hannah said behind him. "Our last day together."

He turned to look at her. He had never seen her so haggard. Her thin face looked all bone; she held onto her cup of tea as if it were her one hope of surviving the morning. He went into the shed and found one of her blankets and put it over her shoulders. Gradually her shivering stopped.

"Thank you, Joey."

"You look tired," he said.

She nodded. "Sometimes it becomes very clear to me that my resources are not unlimited." She smiled faintly. "But today's the big day, Joey. We'll finally get you to your grandparents' house."

He was surprised how litle joy he felt, now that the end of the road was so near. He watched Hannah drink her tea, hoping to see that inner strength return to buoy her up.

"It's the magic, too," she said at last. "It takes a lot out of me. I'll be all right."

They loaded the car, drove out to the main road and started north. No other cars disturbed the peaceful morning. The woods ran along on either side, interrupted occasionally by a farm with its barn and fields, but otherwise presenting two solid walls of greenery. The air was crisp and new, and the sunlight warm and welcome whenever it fell upon them.

The road climbed a ridge, then followed it for several miles above a river valley planted heavily with corn. Joey was amazed at the different shades of green, where one color now revealed itself as a hundred colors. He forgot for a while the sadness he felt that today his travels with Hannah were coming to an end.

The engine, which had been loud all morning, began to make ominous clanking noises as the road led them down toward the valley. At the foot of the hill, when Hannah stepped on the gas, the car lurched ahead with one last fatal barrage, louder than before and more final, and then it died. It jerked to a stop at the side of the road, with smoke pouring from under the hood.

Joey jumped out and lifted the hood, releasing a cloud of black, noxious smoke that burned his eyes. As the smoke gradually cleared, he could discover nothing wrong, until crouching down and looking under the engine, he realized that something was poking out through the oil pan. The last of the oil was dripping away into the sand beneath the car.

"Can we fix it?" Hannah called.

Joey straightened up and shook his head. "It's finished. Looks like a piston rod smashed right out through the oil pan."

Hannah got out and slammed the door. Anger flashed in her eyes, bringing them to life again. "Damn that Tod! I've a good mind to call him collect and tell him to get up here and give me back my money."

Disappointed as he was that the car had failed them, Joey was still happy to see her old spirit return.

"Well, Joey," she said at last, "I guess we'll hike it from here."

"What about all your stuff?"

Hannah shrugged away the look of pain that crossed her face. "Sooner or later I have to let it all go."

"Maybe we can have the car towed into the next town," Joey said. "Then you could store your—"

"No, Joey," Hannah interrupted. "I can't afford to throw good money after bad. It's time to leave it behind, the car and my boxes and my suitcases." She shook her head. "The works."

Hannah walked a short distance up the road, then came back. "There's a side road not too far ahead. We'll push the car in there and set it on fire."

Joey looked at her.

"Well, I'm not going to leave it here so people can pick through my things. Come on, Joey. I'll steer, you push."

Fortunately the road still had a bit of favorable slope left where they had stopped. After making sure Hannah had the engine in neutral, Joey leaned his weight against the back. Slowly, very slowly, the car began to roll ahead. Halfway to the side road, he was able to straighten up and let the car roll on without him. Hannah turned and disappeared behind a wall of scrub spruce trees. He ran to catch up.

When he reached her, she had parked the car in the middle of a sand pit a hundred yards from the main road.

"Lucky for us it was downhill all the way in here," she said. "We could never have pushed it very far in this sand." She began pulling his backpack out of the car. He hurried to help her.

"Are you really going to burn it?"

She nodded. "Dandy morning for a fire." She looked around at the sand hills. "Perfect spot, too."

But Hannah's lighthearted attitude gave way to a different mood as she began going through her things, trying to decide what she could take with her. As she sat in the back of the car, Joey heard her sighing and talking to herself. At one point he thought she began to cry.

Without a word he emptied his own pack and rolled a few essentials in his sleeping bag. He put his mother's photograph in his wallet. With a short length of rope he made a shoulder strap for the sleeping bag. He brought the empty pack to the car.

"Here, put what you can in this."

She looked at him. "What about your things?"

"I don't need most of them anymore."

Slowly she chose what she would keep. He waited a few feet away. A group of crows flew over, cawing rudely.

She came out at last with the pack nearly empty. She went through the glove compartment. The last thing she placed inside the backpack was her leather bag. He helped her close the buckles.

"Can't you take more than this?" he asked.

"I have to carry it. And I have a good distance to go yet."

He swung the pack onto his back and put the new strap of his sleeping bag over his shoulder. She handed him a book of matches.

"Go ahead, Joey."

"You're sure?"

She nodded. "Touch it off. Let's give it a proud farewell."

Hannah had emptied several of her boxes onto the floor of the car. It took several matches to get the cardboard burning. Then he stepped back, and together they watched as the whole interior of the car quickly went to flame. A column of smoke rose in the still air above the sand pit.

"Let's go," Joey said. "Someone may spot it."

Their eyes watered from the heat. Joey took Hannah's arm and led her away. When she stopped one more time to look back, the gas tank exploded, blowing the trunk door several feet from the rest of the car. After that, the fire quickly died away; and by the time they had walked half a mile, all signs of the fire had faded from the morning air.

Joey could hear church bells in the distance, ringing from a village hidden in the hills. As he and Hannah walked, they said very little to each other, but the silence was full of what was unsaid. When the sun was high, they sat in the shade of a half-dead maple tree and finished the last of the crackers, washed down with water from the canteen.

"I could eat two steaks," Joey said.

"Perhaps your grandmother will cook you one tonight."

"I'm not going to my grandparents'," Joey told her. "I'm going with you."

Hannah shook her head. "No, Joey. I have one way to go now and you have another."

"But you can't carry the pack. It's heavy and . . ."

121

"I've done harder things," she told him. She patted his knee. "Besides, I'll get rides. It's a kind offer, Joey, but it's one I can't accept."

"Why not?"Joey looked away, his eyes stinging with tears he wanted to hide.

Hannah sighed. "The book dealer in Hollington told me about a woman in upstate New York who has some of the oldest of the forbidden books, black books dating back to the early days of printing. I'm going there, Joey, to see what she has, to see if she'll share them with me."

"So, I'll go there with you."

"Well, you really can't, Joey. Besides, I've a feeling your grandparents are impatiently awaiting you." She closed the pack and pushed it over to him. "You can carry this for me a little farther, but then you must go to what waits for you, and I to what waits for me."

They walked on through the noontime stillness. A few white clouds appeared and marched in formation across the deep sky. When the road forked, Hannah took the map from the backpack and showed Joey where they were.

"The road to the right leads into Carverville in about eight miles. Just stay on it and you'll be there long before dark."

When he put down the pack, she took hold of his shoulders in her thin hands and studied his face. He met her eyes, then looked away.

"Listen, Joey. I've come to know you well in these few days we've been together. You have a goodness in you that isn't pretense, that isn't fake. Guard it, preserve it. It can guide you." She squeezed his shoulders hard. "I know it's love you're looking for and it's love you must find. And you will."

She let go of him then and took her leather bag out of the

backpack and opened it. She searched through it until finally she brought out a copper-colored medal on a fine silver chain. She squinted at the medal in the sunlight. On one side it was engraved with several intersecting lines within a faint circle, like spokes in a wheel.

"I think this is the right one," she said, half to herself. "Or is this the one to ward off warts?" She pondered awhile, then shook her head. "I don't perfectly remember, Joey, but I'm fairly sure this is the talisman for love. In any case, you can carry it to remember me by."

She dropped the chain over his head. The medal felt warm against his chest.

"Good-bye, Joey."

He hugged her, then helped her put on the backpack. He adjusted the straps for her.

"Good-bye, Hannah," he whispered.

She struck off along the left-hand turn in the road and he along the right. For the first few hundred feet he could see her growing smaller in the distance, then the trees intervened and she was gone.

19

The town of Carverville consisted of a garage and a grocery store, four houses and an abandoned school. The afternoon wind rippled through the grass that grew onto the main street of town. Flowers in front of one of the houses bobbed their heads. Near the garage, the air reeked of gasoline.

Joey walked through the town in five minutes. As the road continued on, he followed the signs for Lake Magogaway. Already he could imagine that the gentle wind brought to him the smell of the lake, the perfume of the wild flowers that he remembered along its shores.

But when he reached the lake, he saw that his grandparents' house was smaller than he remembered it: not as grand, not as white as the picture in his mind.

The house was a center-chimney Cape, with a rusting metal roof, a granite front stoop, and a lawn in back that ran down to the water's edge. The grass needed cutting. A shutter beside one window swung slowly in the wind, banging lightly whenever it touched the house.

For a bad moment or two Joey thought the house was empty, but then he saw his grandfather sitting in a lawn chair beneath the trees in back.

As Joey crossed the lawn, his legs seemed made of sponge. He thought he might never cover the distance that separated him from the figure in the chair. He felt entangled in a dream, a dream that might go on forever. The wind brushed through the trees and softly fanned his face; beyond the lawn, small waves splashed on the beach as if to laugh at everything.

"Granddad," Joey called, to break the spell. "Granddad, it's me, Joey."

His grandfather was asleep, wrapped in a blanket that did not hide the bones of his tall frame. Joey was surprised to see how much he had aged in the two years since they had last seen each other. His hair now was totally white, his face gaunt.

"Granddad?" Joey whispered.

The old man stirred, opened his eyes and looked at him without recognition. "Who are you?"

"Joey, Granddad. You remember me. I'm Joey."

The old man's eyes looked troubled for a moment, then came to life as he smiled. "Joey, it's Joey." He opened up his arms and Joey knelt down into his embrace. The old man patted his back again and again.

"Martha!" he shouted. "It's Joey. Joey's here. Martha!"

When his grandmother appeared through the back door of the house, she was drying her hands in her apron. She was still as plump as Joey remembered her, her gray hair still pinned up in a bun atop her head, the knuckles of her hands red and swollen from water and work. She held him tightly for a moment, then pushed him back to look at him.

125

"Goodness, Joey, you've grown."

"He's a big boy, Joey is," his grandfather said. "He's a big boy."

"Now, Charles, don't get all excited," his grandmother said, straightening the old man's blanket. "You go back to your nap while I fix Joey some supper."

She took Joey to the kitchen, where he sat on a stool and watched her finish off a pie and begin frying chicken.

"I'll put this piece in the oven to bake for your grandfather," she said. "He can't eat fried foods anymore."

"Granddad is . . ."

"He's changed since last you saw him, Joey." She rolled the chickens in flour, then placed it in the hot frying pan. "He's had a couple of strokes. Seems like the fire just went out of him after Jeanne . . . after your mother died. Then when he had to retire from the power company, well, it was just like they told him, go on, get old now, we don't need you anymore."

She shook away the bitterness that had crept into her voice and smiled at him. "But tell me what took you so long to get here. When your father called us Tuesday night to say you'd run off and might be headed here, I just naturally assumed you were, what with the letter you sent. I only just got the letter Tuesday morning, hadn't even had time to answer it when your father called."

She paused to catch her breath. "So we've been expecting you every day, and I must confess we've been getting worried since Friday."

Joey wanted to ask her now if he could stay, but he was afraid she might say no. He quickly told her some of what had happened to him, leaving out any mention of the magic or the adventures in Abaddon Woods and Hollington, for fear she would not believe him. Already, much that had hap-

126

pened during his week with Hannah seemed unreal even to him, as if he'd dreamed it.

"That Hannah sounds like a nice lady," his grandmother said. She began turning the pieces of chicken. "Too bad her car had to break down like that. She could have stayed here and rested for a night before she went on." She put down the tongs and wiped her hands again on her apron. "I hope you thanked her for her help."

Joey smiled. He fingered the medal Hannah had given him.

His grandmother was staring at him. "Now don't tell me, Joey, you didn't even thank her?"

"I did." Joey said. "Of course I did."

They ate in the kitchen as the long shadows from the trees stretched across the lawn to reach the house. Joey tried not to watch as the food fell from his grandfather's lips, only half of it ever reaching his mouth.

"Joey's here," his grandfather kept saying, his gaze dancing happily from Joey to his wife and back again. "Joey's here at last."

While Joey washed the dishes, he heard his grandmother making a phone call. He knew she was calling his father, even though her words were drowned out by the television in the front room, where his grandfather sat alone. When she came back into the kitchen, she wouldn't meet his eyes.

Later, as he helped her make up the bed in the attic room, he asked her if he could stay.

She slowly shook her head. "I told your father to let you spend the week here with us. I told him this was the least we could do for you after coming all that way. Besides, we have to get acquainted all over again, it's been so long." Her false heartiness died in the still attic air.

"But I can't stay," Joey said softly.

"I wish I could say yes, Joey." She dropped the pillow she was holding and put her arms around him. "But you've seen your grandfather. He's not well. He's about all I can handle right now."

"I could help you," Joey said. "I can take care of myself, and I could help you with Granddad."

She shook her head. "We're too old for you to be happy here. Besides, Joey, your place is with your father. I don't know what the trouble is between you two, but I do know he's a good man."

Joey sat down on the edge of the bed and stared out the window behind his grandmother, at the sky that was red with sunset.

"Don't you think you should try to work this out with your father?"

Joey shrugged. "I don't know if I can."

She looked at his sleeping bag. "We'll see tomorrow if we can't find you some clothes. You didn't come with much." She stopped at the door and gazed back at him. "Your father asked about a dog. I told him you didn't have one with you."

"I don't."

"Well, he did seem relieved that you didn't have it anymore." She paused. "Won't you come down and watch television with us?"

Joey looked up at her and nodded. "In a little while."

When she was gone, Joey reached for the medal on the chain around his neck. He wanted to tear it off, throw it into the farthest, darkest corner of the attic. But the chain was surprisingly strong and wouldn't break, and then he changed his mind and dropped the medal inside his shirt again.

Maybe Hannah's magic was all make-believe. Just the

same, he never wanted to forget her, and the medal she had given him would remind him of her for the rest of his life. He imagined that the medal still felt warm on his skin as he pressed it hard against his chest. Remembering Hannah was the most important thing right now.

20

During the week at his grandparents' house, Joey ran every day, on a path that led around the lake, through fields of unmowed grass, into groves of white birch trees. He ran to forget himself and to find himself, after the week during which he had been too busy traveling to run. He established the rhythm again quickly, and his grandfather watched him run and cheered him on.

In the afternoons he sat out in the backyard with his grandfather and played checkers. Sometimes Joey let the old man win, then patiently listened while he taught Joey for the tenth time the same tricks he had taught him earlier in the day, or the day before. The sun shone every day, and the wind each afternoon blew over the lake, and always the little waves ran in upon the gravel beach to break in curls of foam.

"Joey's going to stay," his grandfather said one afternoon when all three of them were playing cards.

Joey's grandmother shook her head. "No, he can't, Charles," she said. "I told you that before."

"Joey's staying," the old man insisted and began to cry.

Joey helped his grandmother weed her vegetable garden. He mowed the lawn and clipped the shrubs. He thought she might misunderstand and think he was trying in this way to get her to change her mind, so he pretended to be feeling all right about leaving at the end of the week. He painted the back shed and told her would come back next summer to paint her whole house.

On Friday it rained briefly. He and his grandfather did not get outside until afternoon, when the sun broke through the clouds and drew water from the wet ground in streamers of mist. They went for a walk together on the path around the lake. To entertain him, Joey turned handsprings, which he had learned in gym class at school. When the medal fell out of his shirt and caught the sun, his grandfather noticed it.

"What's that, Joey?"

Joey stood up and held the medal out on its chain so that his grandfather could examine it.

"It's lovely," the old man said. "It's lovely. What's it for, Joey?"

"To ward off warts," Joey told him. They laughed and later his grandfather insisted he show the medal to his grandmother.

"It's for warts," the old man told her. "It protects Joey from warts."

Joey's father arrived late Saturday afternoon. Joey watched his car approach, then walked slowly around front as the car pulled into the driveway. His father got out and nodded.

"Hello, Joey."

"Hello."

"You gave us all a good scare." His father shook his head as if that wasn't what he wanted to say. "I was worried."

"I'm sorry. I didn't want you to worry."

His father stared at him, then turned to greet the others. Joey's grandmother hugged him, but his grandfather refused to shake hands. Joey watched his father try to deal with the old man's hostility. He wanted to explain, wanted to tell his father that his grandfather was angry because he had come to take Joey away. But the words wouldn't come. He was seeing his father from a great distance, even while they stood only a few feet apart.

At supper the conversation was strained. Joey's grandfather had more trouble than usual handling his food. It fell in pieces around his plate. Joey watched his father try to ignore this.

"Well, tell me, Joey," his father said, "what happened to the dog?"

Joey got up and walked outside. His grandfather followed him. Silently they stood side by side and watched a flock of birds dart over the water in the fading light. Back in the kitchen his father's voice was loud, angry. Joey took the old man's hand and they walked down to the beach.

"Don't go," the old man said. "Stay here, Joey. Stay with me."

Joey picked up a rock and spun it out over the water, where it skipped three times before settling below the surface. "I'll be back next summer, Granddad," he said. "Next summer I'll come for another visit."

In the dim light he couldn't see his grandfather's eyes.

"I'll be back," he repeated. "You'll wait for me to come back next summer, won't you, Granddad?"

But the old man didn't answer. Joey watched him walk in his shambling gait back toward the house. Later, when Joey went in, his grandfather had already gone to bed.

In the morning his grandmother pressed a loaf of warm bread and a bag of cookies into his hands as she kissed him good-bye. Joey waited as long as he could for his grandfather to appear.

"He feels bad that you're going," his grandmother told him. "I guess he's not coming out."

As he climbed into the car, Joey took one last look at the house and thought he saw his grandfather behind the curtains in one window. He waved, just in case.

His father started the car and drove out to the road.

"Be sure to write, Joey!" his grandmother called. "And remember your promise to come back next summer to paint the house."

He shouted good-bye and waved until a curve in the road took them out of sight.

"They're good people," his father said. He stepped on the gas and the town of Carverville came into sight. It was gone in a moment or two.

Joey nodded.

His father fumbled for a cigarette, then put the pack away without taking one. "Got to quit these again," he said. He glanced at Joey. "You have a good tan."

"Yeah."

"Going to tell me about your adventures?"

"I will."

His father coughed. The countryside sped by them. "No rush," he said finally. "I imagine you've got some good stories to tell."

Joey settled back into his seat. "Yeah, I do."

The day was warm, the sky covered by a high overcast that glared in their eyes as they drove south. Traffic was heavy when they reached Route 91. His father moved the car into the right-hand lane, and they matched speed with the cars ahead.

Joey sensed that the silence stretching on between them needed to be broken, needed to be overcome. But the longer it lasted the harder it was to say something, to say anything. The patching up between them was hard to begin; perhaps, he thought, because something more than patching up was needed.

The traffic grew heavier the farther south they drove. In the afternoon, when they turned onto Route 89, the cars were bumper-to-bumper, as tightly wedged into the passing lane as in the right-hand travel lane. Joey amused himself by seeing how many different license plates he could spot. He squinted into the glare, fighting a headache.

When he saw the hitchhiker in the breakdown lane, he had just a glimpse as they drove by of a girl in jeans and a sweater, standing beside a tattered backpack.

"Stop for her?" he asked. "Please?" Memories of his own attempts to hitch rides before he met Hannah were still fresh in his mind.

His father was slowing down. "I don't know, Joey. She's a long way back."

"We can still stop. It's tough trying to get a ride. Nobody wants to stop."

His father pulled into the breakdown lane. By the time Joey could get out of the car, the girl was nearly out of sight behind them. He waved to her, then waved again when she seemed to look their way.

"She's not coming," his father said. "Probably didn't see us stop."

"No, she spotted us." Joey waved again and saw the girl pick up her backpack and begin running toward them. Cars whined by them in a blur. His eyes burned from the dust they blew along with them.

"Here she comes," he said happily. With someone else in the car, maybe they would start to talk and the terrible silence between them would be broken, at least for a while.

The girl ran up to their car. She looked twenty, perhaps a year or two older. Her long brown hair was tied behind her head with a piece of ribbon. She smiled as she greeted him, her dark eyes darting with happiness.

"Thanks for stopping. I thought I'd never get a ride."

He held the door for her as she threw her pack onto the back seat, then climbed in after it. As his father drove ahead in the breakdown lane, trying to find a gap in the traffic, the girl lay against the back seat, catching her breath.

"This is my father," he told her. "I'm Joey."

The girl nodded. "I'm Annie Kimble." She reached out to shake his hand. Her grip was firm, her fingers strong. "I'm going to Boston."

"So are we," Joey told her. "We can give you a ride all the way."

She nodded happily. "It was kind of you to stop," she told his father.

"Well, I've been on the road myself," Joey said, then blushed when he realized how pompous he sounded. "I mean, I know what it's like to hitch rides."

Annie Kimble laughed. "Do you now, Joey? You're a little young to be roaming around on the loose, aren't you?"

When he shrugged, she laughed again.

"And how many young girls' hearts did you break when last you were on the road, Joey?"

He blushed more darkly and didn't answer. The sound of her laughter troubled him, as if he had heard it somewhere before.

135

21

Late in the afternoon they left the highway to find a restaurant. They each ordered something light, then sat trying not to look at each other while they waited.

"What part of Boston are you headed for?" his father asked Annie.

"Beacon Hill," she said. "I have some friends there who are going to put me up until I find a place of my own."

"Are you going to be working in Boston or attending school?" Joey's father leaned back as the waitress arrived with their food. Joey yawned and studied his hamburger without interest. He couldn't keep his eyes open.

"I'm going to be looking for work," Annie told them. "I'm qualified to teach music. Maybe I can find a job doing that."

"In the public schools?"

"Perhaps." She looked across at Joey. "He's falling asleep."

Joey shook himself and stretched. "No, I'm not."

"Is it the wallpaper or the company?"

Joey looked at her.

"Just a joke." She laughed softly. Something familiar nibbled at the edge of his mind again. "Do you live in Boston?" she was asking his father.

"Cambridge, actually," his father told her. "But we'll drop you."

Out in the parking lot after they had eaten, Annie suggested she and Joey change places. "You look as if you need a nap, Joey."

He nodded. They put Annie's backpack into the trunk. In the back of the car Joey listened sleepily to their conversation as his father drove onto the highway, until their words faded into a buzz that was finally swallowed up by sleep.

His dreams were too vague to remember. He woke up several times, as the afternoon darkened, as evening came upon them. Each time he woke up, he saw through sleepy eyes that Annie was looking over the seat at him. He felt a need to say something to her; he woke up each time with words on his lips to tell her. But they faded too quickly, and he drifted back to sleep again, still conscious of her eyes upon him.

The last time he woke up, it was late evening. They had stopped in front of a row of brick apartments. He could see an old-fashioned streetlight through the window of the car, and it blurred in his eyes as he started to fall asleep again. As if from far away, he could hear his father getting out and opening the trunk. Then Annie was bending over the seat, her face close to his.

"Joey, wake up." She touched his knee. "Listen, Joey, can you hear me?"

He mumbled something garbled, but it was enough to assure her of his attention, for she went on in a hurried voice.

"Joey, Hannah was right. Listen to me, Joey. The talisman

she gave you will help you find love." She touched his knee again. "Do you understand?"

He tried to sit up, sleep still clinging to him like incoming seas. Annie was at the door, slipping out of the car.

"The talisman is for love, Joey. Remember that."

Then she was gone.

He knew now the truth about her, and he struggled out of the car. "Hannah!" he shouted. "Hannah, wait!"

But she was already running up the steps of the nearest building, her backpack under one arm. At the top she turned toward them and waved. Then she was inside the front hall, and a moment later he heard the buzzer for the inside door. She disappeared from view.

"Hannah, wait, I want to talk to you!" He tried to follow her, but his father grabbed his arm.

"Stop it, Joey. Why are you calling her Hannah? Her name is Annie."

He stood there with his father, trying to understand it all himself, knowing he could never explain it to anyone else.

"Get back in the car," his father said. "It's late."

As they drove toward the river, his father asked him again why he had called the girl Hannah.

For a moment he hesitated, wondering if somehow he could make his father believe. But how could he, when he could hardly believe it himself? He fingered the medal on the chain around his neck. "*The talisman is for love*," the girl had just told him. . . .

It had to be true. He hadn't been dreaming. It had happened, just the way he remembered it. No dream could be this real.

"I really don't understand you sometimes," his father was saying.

"She just reminds me of someone I met," Joey told him. But in the darkness of the car as they crossed the river into Cambridge, he smiled to himself and held the medal very tightly in his hand.

In the garage under their building, after parking the car, his father made no move to get out. When Joey started to open his door, he stopped him.

"Wait, Joey. Before we go up, there are some things I want to say."

Joey waited. In the shadows inside the car he could not see his father's face.

"I just want you to know that I had a lot of time to think while you were gone," his father said. "A lot of time to worry and a lot of time to ask myself questions."

Joey waited for him to go on. In the silence he tried to think of something he himself could say.

"I called Betty when I came home that night and found you gone. When you didn't come home and it got later and later, I thought you might be with her. You weren't, of course, but she had some things to say, and I guess I listened to her for the first time." His father paused for breath. "She told me I didn't deserve you."

"Dad, I . . ."

"No, let me finish. She told me I didn't deserve you, and she's right. I don't. I haven't for a long time now. But I think I can change, if you'll give me a chance. I don't want you to say anything to me now. I just want you to give me some time."

They got out of the car and headed toward the elevators. Joey walked warily beside his father, hardly daring to hope that what he was hearing from him was true, that there might be a chance for a change between them.

As they waited for the elevator, his father laughed. "If

things do work out between us, you can thank Betty. She really let me have it. With both barrels."

"I'll write her a letter, if things work out." Joey felt as if he couldn't breathe.

"You can do better than that," his father said. "She's coming over to dinner tomorrow night."

Joey looked at his father.

"Did you really think I was going to let someone like her get away?"

In the elevator as they rode up to their floor, Joey realized there were tears in his father's eyes. He wasn't sure which of them made the first move, but a moment later they were hugging each other. The elevator stopped; the door opened on their floor.

"Let's go, Joey," his father said. "Let's go home."

They walked down the corridor together, and his father unlocked the door. As it swung open, Joey saw, across the dark living room, the balcony doors and the view of the city they framed. A thousand lights blazed there as they had every night; but for the first time in such a long, long time, there was a promise of light and warmth inside the room, too.